A CANDLELIGHT ECSTASY ROMANCE™

"Janet," he whispered, *"let me love you."*

Yes, she wanted him to. She wanted this feeling to continue, to grow, and she knew Jason could make that happen.

"Let me, Janet," he murmured again. His mouth trailed a burning path of kisses over her ear before he began a sensuous exploration of it with his moist tongue, leaving her breathless and confused.

The cloud of passion lifted from her brain and reality edged in with his words. She was not the type of woman to be swept off her feet by a man of experience. When the morning came, how would she feel about herself if she gave in to the desires of the moment? The answer to that question was clear.

"Don't," she whispered.

CANDLELIGHT ECSTASY ROMANCES™

1 THE TAWNY GOLD MAN, *Amii Lorin*
2 GENTLE PIRATE, *Jayne Castle*
3 THE PASSIONATE TOUCH, *Bonnie Drake*
4 THE SHADOWED REUNION, *Lillian Cheatham*
5 ONLY THE PRESENT, *Noelle Berry McCue*
6 LEAVES OF FIRE, FLAME OF LOVE, *Susan Chatfield*
7 THE GAME IS PLAYED, *Amii Lorin*
8 OCEAN OF REGRETS, *Noelle Berry McCue*
9 SURRENDER BY MOONLIGHT, *Bonnie Drake*
10 GENTLEMAN IN PARADISE, *Harper McBride*
11 MORGAN WADE'S WOMAN, *Amii Lorin*
12 THE TEMPESTUOUS LOVERS, *Suzanne Simmons*
13 THE MARRIAGE SEASON, *Sally Dubois*
14 THE HEART'S AWAKENING, *Valerie Ferris*
15 DESPERATE LONGINGS, *Frances Flores*
16 BESIEGED BY LOVE, *Maryann Young*
17 WAGERED WEEKEND, *Jayne Castle*
18 SWEET EMBER, *Bonnie Drake*
19 TENDER YEARNINGS, *Elaine Raco Chase*
20 THE FACE OF LOVE, *Anne N. Reisser*
21 LOVE'S ENCORE, *Rachel Ryan*
22 BREEZE OFF THE OCEAN, *Amii Lorin*
23 RIGHT OF POSSESSION, *Jayne Castle*
24 THE CAPTIVE LOVE, *Anne N. Reisser*

FREEDOM TO LOVE

Sabrina Myles

A CANDLELIGHT ECSTASY ROMANCE™

for Ruth
with affection

Published by
Dell Publishing Co., Inc.
1 Dag Hammarskjold Plaza
New York, New York 10017

Copyright © 1981 by Lois A. Walker

All rights reserved. No part of this book may be
reproduced or transmitted in any form or by any
means, electronic or mechanical, including photocopying,
recording or by any information storage
and retrieval system, without the written permission
of the Publisher, except where permitted by law.

Dell ® TM 681510, Dell Publishing Co., Inc.

Candelight Ecstasy Romance™ is a trademark of
Dell Publishing Co., New York, New York.

ISBN: 0-440-12530-8

Printed in the United States of America

First printing—October 1981

Dear Reader:

In response to your enthusiasm for Candlelight Ecstasy Romances™, we are now increasing the number of titles per month from two to three.

We are pleased to offer you sensuous novels set in America, depicting modern American women and men as they confront the provocative problems of a modern relationship.

Throughout the history of the Candlelight line, Dell has tried to maintain a high standard of excellence, to give you the finest in reading pleasure. It is now and will remain our most ardent ambition.

> Vivian Stephens
> Editor
> Candlelight Romances

CHAPTER 1

Janet looked up from the paper she was reading. She had asked her students to write about what they wanted to do when they grew up and, in typical third-grade fashion, over half of them had said they wanted to be rich and not have to do anything.

Don't we all, she thought with amusement as she put aside the last paper and took off her tinted glasses. She looked up in surprise as the door to the empty classroom opened and a tall man in a red plaid cotton shirt and jeans, carrying a stetson hat, walked in.

She was even more surprised when he started to speak. His words were clipped and he seemed almost angry.

"Are you Miss Matthews?" he demanded.

"Yes," she answered.

"You look rather young to be a teacher," he said with a skeptical perusal of her.

"I assure you I am old enough," she replied with cool politeness. "How may I help you?"

"I'm Jason Stewart, I understand you wished to talk with me about my niece, Susan Stewart."

Janet assessed the stranger with a sweeping look. He was a very attractive man in a rugged, outdoor way. His tanned face was lean and alert and matched the suppleness of his tall frame. Below his windswept brown hair were eyes as blue as a cloudless sky—as blue but not nearly as pleasant.

"Is that right?" he demanded as he walked toward her. His long strides brought him quickly to her side. He stopped, towering over her desk.

"That's correct," she replied.

"What about?" he asked curtly, leaning casually back against the blackboard. He looked like a giant in her land of third-grade desks.

Janet swiveled her chair around to face him fully. "I wanted to discuss your niece, Susan. She is having some problems adjusting to her life here, I believe."

"The housekeeper tells me she brought home A's and B's on her last report card," he countered defiantly.

"That's true; her grades are good. Susan's difficulties are not entirely in the classroom although they are manifested there as well. They are mainly in her relationships with the other children. She is painfully shy." Janet paused for Jason Stewart to make some statement. When he did not, she continued. "I believe she should do some work this summer to overcome her timidity. I think it would be good if she became involved in some activities, and professional counseling should not be overlooked. If I may make a suggestion—"

"You may not," he interrupted irritably, pushing himself away from the blackboard and walking toward her. He rested the palms of his hands on the desk top and leaned forward to fix Janet with a level gaze. "I am a busy man, Miss Matthews. I was under the impression you called me in to discuss my niece's schoolwork. As her teacher I am willing to listen to you on that subject, but I am not interested in your hackneyed, pseudopsychological evaluations. When I want your advice on how to raise a child, I'll ask. Considering that you look awfully damn young yourself, I don't think I'll be asking."

His manner was as rude as any she had ever encountered, but she controlled her anger as she replied with dignity. "I think you should ask someone. Susan is going through a very difficult time. Not only has she recently lost her parents, but she has been sent all the way from New Jersey to the wilds of Oklahoma to live with an uncle she had never seen before. I don't wonder she is having problems adjusting."

"You're quite familiar with the family history, aren't you, Miss Matthews? Is genealogy another of your hobbies?" he asked sardonically. "I suggest you control your tendency to pry."

"Your niece told me that herself with no prompting on my part," she told him levelly.

Jason Stewart appeared to have lost interest in the conversation. Putting his stetson hat on, he walked to the door before turning back to her. "Since there seems to be nothing more to say, I'll just be on my way." He gave a brief nod as he touched his hat to her and walked out the door.

Janet sat staring at the open door with a mixture of exasperation and anger. She had known when she became a teacher there were frustrations inherent with the job. But she had expected them to be with the students, not with a parent or guardian. She sighed as she stood and carefully brushed the pleats of her kelly green linen skirt. She smoothed down her mint green blouse before putting papers into her briefcase. She had tried to help Susan, she consoled herself as she walked to the door and stopped outside to lock it. But without the help of the little girl's uncle, there was nothing she could do. Resigned to that thought, she continued down the empty hall to the front doors and stepped out into the heat.

Janet proceeded homeward slowly, looking around at the numerous flowers as she walked the two blocks to her small rented house. The remembrance of her interview with Jason Stewart was still fresh in her mind and she found herself considering it again. He was not the first person she had met in western Oklahoma who did not take kindly to advice. The local people seemed to have a great deal of what they considered rugged pioneer spirit. Janet privately thought the trait was more commonly called stubbornness. At any rate, she had had more than one discussion with a parent that had ended on a sour note. Her suggestions were deemed meddling. They had been called as much by one indignant mother when Janet hinted her child's problems in school were due partially to a hearing difficulty.

"Nobody in my family ever had hearing trouble," the woman had roared. Janet had been sorely tempted to agree that was probably true at home if the whole clan spoke at such a volume. But she had said nothing further. In a tiny school which had no nurse, she knew there were many emotional and physical problems that went undetected. She was limited in the help she could give. If her suggestions were ignored, there was little else she could do.

"Hello, Janet," a voice surprised her.

Looking up, Janet saw a stooped, gray-haired woman coming toward her.

"Hi, Bessie," she greeted her neighbor.

"Hot, ain't it?" The old woman looked up at the sky, shielding her eyes with her hand. "Going to get really hot this summer. Here it is only May and it's already in the midnineties. You're probably not used to such heat."

Janet smiled. Indiana was not in the arctic zone, but the way people in this state spoke of it, they must think it was.

"I'm sure I can bear it," she said lightly.

"You won't be going home for the summer?" Bessie asked.

"No, I'm staying in Freedom when school lets out."

The woman shook her head. "Not much happens here in the summer," she warned.

Janet laughed. She didn't doubt that because not much occurred in the other three seasons. "I have plenty of books to read and I can always drive to Alva to the library or a movie. I think I'll enjoy the solitude."

"Well, come down if you get bored," Bessie told her and started back toward her white frame house.

"I will," Janet replied, and walked past the three houses which separated her from her own little stucco house. It *was* hot today, but heat had never bothered her. Besides, when school let out next week, she could stay inside in the air-conditioning if it became unbearable. She smiled to herself in anticipation of the upcoming vacation—three months of freedom.

"Freedom," she repeated aloud in amusement. When she had decided to quit her teaching job in

Indiana and move out of state, she had had a choice of three jobs. Two of them were in Chicago schools and would have paid more money, but she had picked this town in western Oklahoma because she had been attracted by the name—Freedom.

The town was as open and unencumbered as its name. It was set in the middle of a flat valley with picturesque buttes outlined against the sky on one side. It was a tiny rancher's village with a commercial district only two blocks long. The business street was flanked by a grid of avenues containing about seventy houses of stucco and frame.

Meandering beside Freedom was the Cimarron River, a sand-choked riverbed that carried the merest trickle of a stream most of the year. Only in the flood season did the whirling water rush through the wide channel in a ruthless pathway to the sea.

Some years ago a town merchant had conceived an idea to make Freedom look like an authentic western town in the hope of attracting more tourism. Not that Freedom, with its population of 292, had much to offer tourists, but the townspeople had not fully considered that and they had adopted the plan with a relish. The result was that all the buildings on Main Street now had old-fashioned straight storefronts of unpainted wood. The tumbleweed that occasionally drifted down the wide street completed the effect.

Janet liked Freedom, she decided, as she stepped inside the door of her one-bedroom rented house and set her briefcase down. Sinking onto the red and blue Early American sofa, she put her feet up on the maple coffee table and continued thinking about the circumstances that had brought her here.

After the deaths of her parents and her fiancé, it

had seemed important to leave Bloomington and the rambling old Victorian house, the scene of her childhood. Ever since she could remember her mother and father had rented a room to foreign students. But when Lars had moved in, she had known that he was different.

Lars. Janet remembered him with a sigh. He had been a handsome Scandinavian who accented his words in the most unexpected places with a charming result. She had been captivated by his Nordic good looks, blond and carefree, and his easy smile. He was working on his doctorate in biochemistry and she was teaching in a local grade school when they met. Although she no longer lived at home, she had suddenly found a great many reasons to stop by the house, and she saw a great deal of Lars. Gradually they became a couple and in the middle of his second year in the States they became engaged. Lars only had a few months left to complete his thesis and he had already landed a job teaching biochemistry at a university in Sweden. Their future was secure.

Janet was learning the language and searching for a job in an American school in Sweden. It had been an exciting time for her—full of happy plans for the future. Then, things had gone terribly wrong. Her fiancé and her parents had died when a heater in the old Victorian house malfunctioned. They had all been asphyxiated in their sleep.

It was then that Janet discovered her apartment wasn't far enough across town from the empty house which had been her home. So she had looked for another job, one that would offer her a new setting in which to start over.

When she told the placement counselor she would

like a position out of state, he informed her of two in Chicago, mentioning the one in Oklahoma only as an afterthought. But as soon as Janet heard the name of the town, she had made her decision. It might not be the place to spend a lifetime, but she hoped it would provide a new setting where she could sort out the tattered pieces of her life.

Freedom, she learned soon after her arrival, was anything but a drawing card for college graduates. The school had had a hard time keeping teachers the past few years, especially young ones. When Janet arrived last September, she had been determined to stay at least for the school year. And she had.

She came back to the present with the realization she had forgotten to stop at the store on her way home. Since she was out of both milk and bread, the trip was essential. Picking up her purse, she started out the door toward the town's one grocery. It was only a block away, at the end of the two-block stretch of shops which included a bank, a hardware store, a drugstore, two restaurants, and the volunteer fire station. She covered the distance in a short time and picked up the items she needed. Then she carried them to the checkout counter where an elderly woman was engaged in conversation with the checker. Janet prepared to wait patiently. She had learned her first month in town that the grocery was the social hub of Freedom. It was not uncommon to be delayed a few minutes while the local gossip was exchanged.

As she waited, a child's voice behind her drew her attention. "Look, Uncle Jason, there's Miss Matthews."

Janet turned to the customers standing in line behind her to see Jason Stewart and Susan. The little girl smiled shyly at her and Janet returned a warm smile before addressing Susan's uncle. "Hello, Mr. Stewart," she said in a pleasant voice.

He responded to her greeting with the barest nod of his head.

Susan appeared unaware of any undercurrent between the adults as she continued, "Isn't she pretty, Uncle Jason? Just like I told you." Then, self-conscious at having said so much, her face turned a delicate shade of pink and she looked down at the floor.

"Thank you, Susan," Janet said. "I'm flattered and a little embarrassed." Her words were calculated to draw attention from the little girl and make her feel more at ease. They worked, for Susan looked up quickly.

"Why should you be embarrassed?" she asked innocently. Turning to her uncle, she continued, "I think she has the nicest brown eyes. For an older woman she looks very well preserved."

At those words, Jason broke into a laugh and Janet smiled. The customer in front of her left and she moved up to pay for her own purchases. After giving the correct change, she started for the door.

"Good-bye, Miss Matthews," Susan called.

Janet turned back and smiled. "Good-bye, Susan. Mr. Stewart," she added with a polite but distant nod.

He *was* handsome, she conceded as she started back to her house. It was too bad he didn't have more of a yielding disposition; it was doubtful that he ever went out of his way to gain anyone's approval. That might account for why he was still single at thirty-five, Janet thought with a wry smile, recalling another fact which had been related by Susan.

Stepping back into her house, Janet crossed to the kitchen and put the milk into the refrigerator. A small chuckle escaped her as she remembered Susan's words—"for an older woman." Being an unmarried schoolteacher, she realized, must make her seem like a decrepit spinster to her students. And her age, even though she looked far younger, was a walloping twenty-six. To any seven-year-old that must be sure confirmation of senility.

If she stayed in Freedom, Janet knew she would remain single because there weren't many eligible men. In fact, there were very few males in the town *period*. Most of them lived out on the sprawling ranches which surrounded the town, and she had no way of meeting them.

Janet poured a glass of milk and walked back into the living room, settling herself onto the couch as her thoughts continued to drift.

Men. In the past few months they had become only a peripheral part of her life. The ones she had dated before Lars had receded to the back of her mind when she met him. But he had been dead nearly a year now and she knew it was time she made an effort to form new relationships with members of the opposite sex.

It had never been hard for Janet to meet men; her looks had attracted a great many. It was not that she was beautiful—she wasn't. But she was pretty, and she had a vivacity men seemed to find appealing. Janet wasn't vain about her looks, but she was confident of them and pleased with her small features accented with soft brown eyes and a mouth that held the faint upward curve of a ready smile.

She finished the last of her milk and set the glass down. So much for considering her looks, she thought with a smile. It scarcely made any difference how gorgeous she was if there was no one to use her fatal charms on. Well, she decided, in view of the fact her social life was nonexistent it was probably safe to leave the phone and drive over to Alva and take in a movie.

Janet walked from the living room into the small bedroom and looked through her closet for something to wear. She pulled out a pair of white slacks and a blue knit top and changed from her skirt and blouse into the more casual attire. Then she brushed her hair from its natural center part to the soft curls at her shoulder. Taking a navy blue sweater from the drawer of the oak waterfall dresser, she slung it over her shoulder.

Moments later, in her red compact car, she started for Alva. As she drove north down the straight road, she passed ranch-style houses set amidst the cactus, sagebrush, and salt cedar. Behind her, in the rear view mirror, she could see the 150-foot high cliffs of red sandstones and shales that bordered the river before spreading out into the badlands behind. The scenery was both serene and stark. It gave her a secure feeling to know the landscape had stood with little change for thousands of years. It must appear now much as it had looked when it belonged to the Indian and the buffalo.

In places, of course, modern civilization had left a heavy mark. Alva, a town of 7500, was the cattle and cultural center for a 100-mile radius. Farther east, the giant city of Enid boasted 50,000 souls. Its huge grain elevators rose high into the sky and were visible for miles across the flat plains.

Janet's attention was focused sharply back onto the road as a large drill truck passed her small car, shaking it like a leaf in the wind. The truck was a sign of the oil which lurked everywhere beneath the surface.

As she drove into the fringes of Alva, Janet passed the cluster of brick buildings of Northwestern State University and turned left toward the center of town. There she spent an hour at the library and some time in a dress shop deliberating between two blouses. She only had time for a quick supper before she hurried over to the theater.

Janet didn't even notice what picture was playing as she paid the attendant. It didn't really matter to her. Tonight she just wanted to be out of her house and among people.

She walked inside the theater, took a seat in a middle row, and settled back on the red velvet chair. She glanced around the quaint old hall that was complete with a balcony in the rear and a stage for vaudeville acts. Lining the walls were Tiffany-style wall sconces and from the ceiling old-fashioned fans gently stirred the air.

Janet was distracted from her appreciation of the movie house as she felt something soft glance off the back of her head. She turned in surprise to see half a dozen teen-age boys lined up two rows behind her. They were grinning and nudging each other. One of them held a piece of popcorn poised in his hand. Obviously it was the means they had used to gain her attention. She turned back to face the screen but she could hear their words as they discussed her.

"Hey, Doug, why don't you go put the make on her?"

"Make your move, man," another voice added.

Janet sat stiffly in her seat. Their speech was slightly slurred, indicating they probably had been drinking. To change seats would only call more attention to her and there was nothing to prevent their moving along with her. But, she realized, if she stayed, they could very well move down and sit with her here.

As that thought flashed through her mind, one of them put it into action. Just as the house lights went down, a husky boy staggered into a vacant seat beside her and put his arm casually around her shoulder.

"Go get her!" and "Atta boy, Doug," he was encouraged from behind.

Janet shrugged his arm off and turned to him indignantly. "I suggest you leave."

"Why?" he demanded. As he spoke, his hand moved companionably back around her shoulder. "I'll stay and we can get acquainted," he leered.

The credits began to roll across the screen and the music played, but Janet was aware only of his hard grip and the strong smell of whiskey.

She wasn't exactly afraid; they *were* in a public place even if the theater was almost empty. But she was annoyed. She stood to leave, but before she could move farther, he yanked her back into the seat. Janet hesitated. There was a very simple way she could deflate his ardor if worst came to worst but she hated to take such a step until it was absolutely necessary.

While she paused in indecision, a tall, shadowy form appeared and pulled the boy out of the seat.

Holding him by the collar of his shirt, the man spoke in a terse voice. "I don't think the lady wants your company." He released the teen-ager abruptly. The boy gave a final uncertain look at Janet before creeping back to sit sullenly with his friends. The man slid into the vacant chair beside her, giving Janet her first clear view of him.

"Mr. Stewart!" she breathed in surprise.

"Yes," he answered shortly. "I thought you might need some help ridding yourself of Romeo."

"I had a trick or two up my sleeve," she whispered, "but your method was more refined. Thank you."

He made no reply, merely staring ahead at the movie. He had apparently decided to stay to protect her from any further advances.

"I am able to take care of myself," she said, but when he did not answer, she desisted and turned to watch the movie. Jason, she saw out of the corner of her eye, was sitting with his long legs resting out into the aisle and his head tilted slightly back. His hands rested on his stomach; he seemed completely at ease, as if he were watching the show alone.

She leaned toward him. "Is Susan with you?"

His eyes flicked from the screen and swept her face. "Hardly," he said dryly. "I don't think this is a film for a child to see; since it's restricted, she couldn't have come anyway. I don't know why your admirers were allowed in."

Janet started to ask him what the movie was, but she stopped. It would look foolish, she realized, to ask such a question. She nonchalantly looked back toward the screen.

The scene that met her eyes there came as a surprise—a not entirely pleasant one. A man and a woman were in bed together, locked in a passionate embrace.

It was a sight which would not have alarmed her terribly had she viewed it alone or with certain other men. Somehow, such casual intimacy was disquieting when seen with Jason Stewart. Judging from what she had viewed so far, it did not appear to be a movie she would enjoy anyway. She picked up her purse from the seat beside her and rose to leave.

Jason looked up. "Need something? Popcorn? Coke?"

"No, I'm not staying," she said and stepped past him. She continued down the darkened aisle and out the front door, glancing back as she realized that someone had followed her. When she saw it was Jason, she turned and addressed him in a brisk voice. "Thank you for your help in ridding me of that pest."

As he looked down at her, the lights of the marquee made his face appear almost wolfish. "Weren't you enjoying the movie?" he asked in a mocking voice.

"Yes, it was very well done," she replied brazenly.

"I'm surprised you could tell," he continued with a derisive laugh. "You didn't stay to watch much of it."

"Thank you for your help," she said coldly. "Good night." Turning, Janet walked off down the street. She knew he was watching her; she could feel his eyes on her, but he did not follow. When she reached her car, she slid in and drove away from the downtown district. The distance she put between herself and Jason Stewart did not succeed in dispelling him from her mind. In fact, she was so preoccupied with him that she didn't even notice the miles rolling by as she sped back to Freedom.

There was something about him that disturbed her. It wasn't just the cool, sardonic way he appraised her; it was a subtler thing she couldn't quite put her finger on. But she was sure no other man had ever affected her in such a manner. It was possible, she considered, that because of her loneliness, she found herself attracted to a man who normally would not have appealed to her. He *was* a strong male, even if he could be very irritating, and maybe he entered her life at a time when she needed such a person. She had always been independent, but recently she had recognized a need to lean on someone —just a little. Even if she saw Jason as that person, she reminded herself, it hardly mattered because she would be seeing very little more of him. If she did see him, it would be quite by accident.

CHAPTER 2

The next few days were busy ones. It was the end of the school year and Janet had papers to grade, meetings to attend, and final tests to make up.

She was relaxing on her lunch break with Lila Randal, the fourth-grade teacher, after a particularly active morning. The two women were the last ones left at the long wooden table in the teachers' lounge. Lila, a pretty brunette with a pleasantly plump figure, was leafing through a magazine while Janet peeled an orange.

"You look beat," the other woman commented, looking up as she turned a page.

"I am a little," Janet admitted. "The students are becoming more rambunctious as the end of the year gets closer. I'm sure you've noticed," she added with a laugh.

"Oh yes," Lila replied. She looked back at her magazine and said casually, "I thought I saw Jason Stewart coming out of your room the other day."

"Yes. His niece is in my class; he came to talk about her."

"I'm surprised at that," Lila observed, looking up with interest.

"Why?" Janet asked curiously.

23

"He's not the type to take the trouble."

"Take the trouble?" Janet repeated in confusion.

"Yes. He owns one of the largest ranches around and he runs it like a first-class business. Anything that can be delegated usually is. His foreman handles most matters. Jason's busy with a million other concerns."

"It was hardly something his foreman could attend to," Janet responded dryly.

"Well, no, but the housekeeper is in charge of Susan, I think, so I would have imagined she would have come."

"He came," Janet said, "although he seemed very resentful. He appeared to think I was meddling in his family matters when I suggested his niece was having difficulty adjusting to life here."

Lila didn't seem surprised by that bit of information. "I'm sure that's what he believed," she affirmed candidly.

"It's my duty as a teacher to bring such a problem to his attention, especially when it is reflected in her classroom performance," Janet said with firm conviction.

"Of course it is. Don't let his attitude bother you," Lila soothed. "I've known him all my life. He's always been wary of people he thinks are prying into his personal affairs. It's possible he even believed the whole meeting was set up just so you could meet him."

"He's not the type of man I'd go out of my way to be introduced to," Janet retorted.

"You're in the minority. Jason was in the grade ahead of me in school and even then girls were after him. One even tried to force him to marry her by claiming he was the father of her child. It turned out the blood type was wrong, but that certainly didn't improve his opinion of women, I'm sure. Of course, I suspect he was soured on our sex even before that. His mother ran away with another man when he was only five; but then Erica Stewart was always wild. Don't get me wrong, Jason's not a woman hater—as his latest could tell you—but he keeps himself aloof. Maybe men in his position have to," she added.

"Humph," Janet murmured. "I feel sorry for his 'latest.'"

"Don't. She's a beautiful blonde from Tulsa who has everything going for her. She flies out to see him pretty frequently."

"Doesn't he ever go see her?" Janet asked.

Lila gave her a shrewd look. "You certainly are interested in his affairs," she observed.

"Idle curiosity," Janet said with a shrug. She applied herself once again to the orange on the table in front of her.

The other woman continued, "Well, naturally, I'm not in his confidence, but I don't think he goes to Tulsa very often. I doubt he'd put himself out that much. He lets the women come to him, takes what he wants, and then sort of drops them."

"I know the type."

"The women who pursue him probably aren't any more in love with him than he is with them," Lila observed. "But let's face it, he *is* good-looking and he does have a lot of money to boot."

"I suppose that would be enough for some women," Janet noted as she stood to leave.

The next day Janet cleared out her desk and stood

up with a contented sigh. It was the last day of the school year and the room was vacant and ready for next year's students. The exuberant shouts of the children outside could be heard through the windows.

Why was it, she wondered with a smile, that they couldn't wait to be dismissed from school for the summer, but when they were finally released, they stayed around the hated building? That, she decided, was another of the mysteries of children. But right now she didn't intend to ponder that enigma. She was going to put the thoughts of her pupils aside and go home to start her own vacation.

Janet walked from the room and stopped to lock up before continuing down the hall and out the front door of the red brick building.

"Miss Matthews!" a child's voice cried as Janet stepped outside.

Janet turned as Susan ran up to her. The child was panting as she wiped a fist across her tearstained face. Her red hair which earlier had been braided in two neat pigtails now hung limply about her face; her green eyes were red-rimmed from crying. Completing the picture of dishevelment, Janet noted that her yellow striped top was smudged with dirt and the knees of her slacks were torn.

"What happened?" she asked with concern.

"I fell down," Susan said and the tears began to flow anew.

"Did you hurt yourself?" Janet knelt beside her.

"No, but I g-got all dirty," Susan moaned.

"There's no need for tears," Janet said bracingly. "Dirt comes out."

"That's not why I'm c-crying. I went to the bathroom to wash and the bus left without me." Her voice trembled on the last words before she broke into noisy sobs.

"Don't cry, Susan. It's not the end of the world. We'll just go to the office and call your uncle to let him know where you are. Then I'll take you home." To dispel Susan's uncertain look, she added briskly. "There's really no problem, is there?"

Susan shook her head in agreement, apparently satisfied that her worries were now in the hands of someone competent to deal with them. Brushing away her tears she trailed after Janet back into the deserted halls of the school building. When they reached the principal's office, it was locked and empty. Janet inserted her key into the door and pushed it open, flipping on the wall switch as she walked in. Susan followed and seated herself on a chair Janet indicated. She looked around curiously while Janet picked up the phone and dialed the number the little girl recited.

A moment later it was answered by a woman with a heavily accented voice. "Is Mr. Stewart there, please?" Janet asked. "This is Miss Matthews and I'm calling concerning his niece."

"One mo-ment, pleese."

Then Jason Stewart's rich-timbred voice came on the line. In the background Janet could hear several other men's voices, as if he were taking the call in the midst of a meeting. "Jason Stewart," he said abruptly.

"This is Janet Matthews. I'm calling about Susan. She missed the bus and I wanted to let you know so you wouldn't worry. I'll be bringing her home shortly."

"Thank you," he said.

Janet's eyes flicked across to the little girl who was seated on a straight backed chair by the wall swinging her legs. On an impulse she added, "Mr. Stewart, would it be all right if—"

"Speak up, please, I can't hear you." His words were loud and clear, but in the background Janet could also hear the swell of other voices. She began again, louder, "I wonder if you would mind if I kept Susan for a while. This is the last day of school and I thought she might want to celebrate by—"

"Miss Matthews," he cut through again. "I really must go. Thank you for calling."

"But what about your niece?" she persisted. "Would it be all right if I didn't bring her home immediately?"

"Yes, whatever you think." His words were harried. "Good-bye."

Janet hung up the phone and turned to Susan. The little girl's face was alight with expectation. "Is Uncle Jason going to let me stay with you for a while?"

"Yes. I have to drive to Alva to return some books. Would you like to go with me?"

"Oh yes!"

Janet smiled. She had thought Susan would enjoy the trip. Most children liked to get out. Janet had to admit her motives were not entirely unselfish. The idea of returning to her empty house after the last day of school seemed oddly unappealing. She was glad to have Susan's company.

All in all, they had a very pleasant outing. After window shopping in Alva, they had a leisurely meal at a small clean café, treating themselves to huge slices of chocolate pie out of proportion to the small hamburgers they had eaten. It was obvious from Susan's appreciation of all she saw that she did not go out very often. Because she was enjoying herself so much, Janet didn't try to hurry her. Consequently, it was after six before they left Alva and it was well past seven before they neared the ranch.

Susan gave directions as they drove up into the rolling badlands that were dotted with tumbleweed, sagebrush, and cactus. Gradually, the hills flattened into a high plateau where the land was farmed in places and cattle roamed the untilled acres.

Janet turned the car down the long, straight road Susan indicated and followed its rocky path for a quarter of a mile to a large house. After stopping in front of a Spanish-style hacienda, she followed Susan across the spacious green lawn toward the front door. As she walked, Janet surveyed the manicured yard and the clean white farm buildings beyond. The house, a white two-story structure with a clay tile roof and domed windows, received her greatest approval. It was a tasteful villa that blended well with its surroundings.

Janet was distracted from her inspection just as she reached the door. It was jerked open to reveal Jason standing in the doorway, looking forbidding and even taller than she had remembered. His eyes burned Janet with a look of disgust before they alighted on Susan.

"Are you all right?" he demanded of the little girl.

"Yes," Susan assured him with a perplexed look.

His eyes scanned her until he seemed to have satisfied himself that she was. "Go along now and watch television. I want to speak to Miss Matthews."

Susan obeyed, darting a quick look at the pair before crossing the living room and disappearing through another door. Janet's eyes moved back to Jason.

His glare was hard and uncompromising. "Well?" he demanded icily.

"Well what?" she answered in a tone to match his own.

"Where have you been?"

"Susan and I went to Alva."

"You did what!" he exploded.

Janet made a gesture of irritation. "I am not going to stand out on your step like a vacuum cleaner salesman and try to talk to you. It's obvious there's been some confusion over our telephone conversation. If you will allow me to come in—" she paused to look at him challengingly, "I can explain everything."

He moved back with sardonic deference to allow her to enter. She walked into a long living room furnished with modern chrome and glass furniture and a sectional sofa and chairs in ocher yellow.

"Follow me," he said curtly, and led her down a wide hall hung with pictures. He stepped into a study paneled in dark wood. It contained two large leather wing chairs and a massive desk. Taking a seat behind the desk, he motioned her to a chair.

When he spoke, his words were grating. "Now, perhaps you would care to explain why you kept Susan so long? Have you any idea what time it is?"

He was angry—so much so that his blue eyes had a metallic glint in them. Janet stared at him in disbelief while a growing sense of outrage coursed through her. Obviously there had been a misunderstanding on the phone, doubtless caused by his inability to hear her clearly. But he had no right to treat her as if *she* were the one in the wrong.

"I have a very nice watch, thank you. I know exactly what time it is," she snapped.

"Then why the hell wasn't my niece home when she should have been?"

"You are shouting," she said quietly, determined to remain cool and in control.

"You're damn right I am!" He leaned forward across the desk to fix her with a malevolent gaze. "I have reason to shout. If you would answer my questions, I wouldn't have to yell like I was talking to some idiot."

Her determination to be rational and calm flickered momentarily, but she controlled her anger and continued in an even voice, "If you will let me speak, Mr. Stewart, I can explain."

He sat back in the leather chair and listened in brooding silence, fixing her with a stare from polar blue eyes.

Janet proceeded. "Susan missed the bus. When I found her, I called you." She stopped and looked at him, as if defying him to dispute her words.

"Go on," he commanded, pushing the chair back and standing to loom above her.

"I telephoned and asked permission to keep Susan and you agreed," she finished logically, rising to face him on a more even level.

"Are you through?" he asked coldly.

"Yes."

"Then you may go." His words were clipped and indifferent.

Janet faced the tall man squarely. "Then you don't admit you were at least partially in the wrong?"

"I do not," he agreed.

Janet studied him in exasperation as she realized rationality was lost on Jason Stewart. Prompted by a desire to jolt him out of his self-complacency, she said sarcastically. "You wouldn't concede you ever made a mistake, would you? I doubt you ever listen to anyone else. The other day when you came to the school and I tried to discuss Susan's problems I didn't get anywhere either."

"Miss Matthews, it is your behavior which is in question here—not mine. Is it the practice of the school to send teachers to the homes of guardians to insult them?" he finished coolly.

"I am not here on behalf of the school system," she retorted.

"No?" he asked with a dangerous softness. "But you do work for them. I think the school board would be interested to know you are going about to people's homes criticizing them. Yes," he continued in the same soft tone, "it might be something I should mention to someone on the board. I know all the members and I don't believe you would be hired for the next school year if they had a complaint from someone with a landholding as large as mine. I do pay taxes on this property, you know, and that goes into the school fund."

Janet felt a wave of trepidation roll over her. Jason Stewart very likely could have her dismissed with a few well-placed words. Freedom was a small town and she didn't doubt his influence in it. With a black mark such as that on her record, Janet knew it would be difficult to get another teaching position. But she was not willing to bend to him. His look of satisfied superiority only made her more stubborn in her refusal to apologize. Tossing her head proudly, she noted, "If it will make you feel better to take your hostility out on me, then go ahead."

"Fine words, but how easy would it be to find another job if you were fired?" he challenged.

Janet straightened. "Do whatever you wish. It is apparent that you will not listen to reason."

"And 'reason' these days is parading around disguised as a teen-age girl?" he asked caustically. Walking around the desk, he looked down at her with an icy stare. "I think there is nothing more to be said. Please leave, Miss Matthews."

There was little to be gained by staying, Janet realized. Without a backward glance, she marched to the door of the study and down the hall to the front door. Moments later, she drove off into the dark desert night.

Everything about her interview with Jason Stewart had been unnerving. And the tension between them, Janet was certain, had been caused by more than a misunderstanding. It was not precisely a personality conflict either. If anything, she would have said they were more attracted to each other than repelled. At least that was true for her.

As she sped through the darkness, she recalled the almost palpable sensuality she felt when she was with Jason Stewart. Why? He was everything she didn't like in a man. He wasn't gentle or understanding and he certainly didn't have any concern for her.

All right, she told herself sternly, *let's analyze this rationally. He is the first really attractive man I've been in close contact with in a very long time. I'm lonely and I'd be vulnerable to any man.* It was an explanation that did not entirely satisfy her. Even taking her loneliness into account, she had never felt such a powerful physical attraction for any other man. She didn't like her feelings to be out of her control—especially not for a person such as Jason.

As she rounded a curve and saw the lights of the town below, Janet put all thoughts of Jason behind her. Any feelings she had for him must be kept in stern check; he was not the sort of person a woman could afford to lose her heart to.

The next morning was the first day of her summer vacation. Janet awoke early and lay back on the bed with a sigh. Through the lacy curtains she could see that it was a beautiful sunny day outside. She debated for a moment whether to lie in bed and savor her freedom to do so or whether to go for a long walk. She opted for the latter choice. Minutes later, dressed in a blue and white checked top and a pair of jeans, Janet started out the door and walked through town to the river.

As she approached it, she considered that the Cimarron was like everything else in the wide open spaces of western Oklahoma—clean and deserted. It looked more like a scene from an old western movie than a place in the twentieth century. As Janet stepped off the asphalt road into the dry sand, she almost felt as if she were leaving civilization behind and returning to another era.

There were no fences in sight and Janet speculated it must look little different than it had in the open range days when cattle barons had waged wars against rustlers. Kicking up a little cloud of dust with one sandaled foot, she walked onward, her mind still held by thoughts of the past. Surely the old west was the place for men like Jason Stewart, a time when his individualism would have fit well.

As she looked up at the clean blue sky, she drifted even further back into the past to a time before humanity. She bent to pick up a handful of sand and let it sift through her fingers as she surveyed the bluffs around her. The brick red cliffs along the river towered upward like the monoliths of Stonehenge—ancient but silent. These cliffs must have witnessed much, Janet considered as she stopped and squinted her eyes upward. Then she slowly resumed her walk.

Her mind was yanked into the present as she rounded a wide bend and stopped in surprise. A large truck was only a few hundred feet ahead of her in the dry river channel. It looked too small to be an oil field rig, but Janet could think of no other reason for it to be in such an unlikely place. Her curiosity drew her forward. Walking in the thick sand was like moving in heavy snow—slow and laborious. By the time Janet covered the distance to the truck, she was out of breath. She paused to rest by the door of the vehicle, leaning slightly against it.

"Hello there," a male voice startled her.

She straightened swiftly to see a man standing near her, smiling at her. His dark hair was almost completely covered by a white hard hat but she could see that he was young. She guessed him to be in his late twenties. He had friendly green eyes even if he was not exactly handsome. His features were too irregular for that epithet, but they were pleasantly interesting.

"What are you doing here?" the stranger asked.

"I was just out for a walk," she explained. Then, as an official-looking emblem caught her eye, she added quickly, "If I'm not supposed to be here, I'll leave."

The man laughed good-naturedly. "Well, *we* have to have a right-of-entry from the landowner to bring a rig in, but I wouldn't think you would need one to walk down the river." His words were disarming and his smile coaxed one back from her.

"Can I ask what you're doing?" Janet ventured a question.

"We're taking core samples of the rock."

"What for?"

"The government is thinking of building a dam here and we need to explore the site before we can make a determination of where to place it."

She looked doubtfully at the thin stream of water running down the middle of the massive, dry channel. "A dam? There's not much water."

"That's true, but it's not an ordinary dam to hold fresh water. This stream is highly polluted with natural salt. The dam would be constructed to hold back the salt water and prevent it from going on downstream."

"Natural salt pollutes the water?" She had somehow come to associate the word *natural* with good. She had never really considered nature harming itself.

"It sure does. I'll show you." He led her around to the back of the drill truck where several wooden boxes were laid out. Inside of them cylinders of red rock were neatly placed. They looked much like the sandstones and shales of the bluffs along the river, but here and there a clear, glassy-looking rock caught the sun and gleamed.

She pointed to a piece of it. "What's that?"

"Gypsum. It's part of the problem, but this one here," he indicated another shiny rock, "is halite—bedded salt—it's the main cause of the pollution."

She looked around with interest. "Where is everyone else? Surely you don't drill this rock all by yourself?"

He laughed. "No, but I'd probably have to if the driller thought he could con me into it. I'm the geologist. The driller and his two helpers have gone into town to get some parts for the rig. In fact, I was just getting ready to run into Freedom myself; I need to make a call to my office."

"Then I won't keep you," Janet said as she turned to leave.

"I'll take you back to town," he offered quickly.

"No, thanks, I'm just out for a stroll so I'm in no hurry to get back." Janet didn't add that she didn't get into vehicles with men she didn't know.

As if he sensed her unspoken objection, he urged. "I work for the government and I'm driving one of their trucks, so I can't be that shady a character. Besides, you know you're tired," he added.

The latter statement was certainly true. She had caught her breath, but her legs ached from the walk and the thought of retracing her steps was not all that appealing. What he said was obviously true; he was wearing a hard hat with an emblem matching the one on the truck and he did seem to know the geology of the area. Surely he could be trusted.

"You'd be doing me a great favor to ride with me;

then I won't have to open the gates," he encouraged her.

She nodded her head decisively. "Okay."

"Good," he said as he swung open the door of the truck for her. Janet slid in on the passenger's side while he walked around and got in the driver's seat.

"How can you drive in such thick sand?" she asked, looking around dubiously.

"It has four-wheel drive. Right now it will go just about anywhere. When it rains, we have to use an all-terrain vehicle with balloon tires," he explained. "By the way, my name's Ron Leonard," he introduced himself as he drove off the sand into a pasture.

"I'm Janet Matthews."

"I'm very glad to meet you," he replied.

Janet smiled. He did seem happy to have become acquainted with her. It was probably just as hard for him to find unattached women in this remote area as it was for her to find men. Fate, she considered with wry humor, had killed two birds with one stone.

He followed a thread of road through the field before emerging moments later at one end of town.

"There were no gates," she teased, suppressing a laugh.

He gave her a sideways glance and a rueful smile, "I know. But I couldn't think of any other thing to say to make you come with me. Mad?"

"No," she answered truthfully. "I'm not sure my legs would have held up on the trip back."

Ron traversed Main Street and stopped in front of the drugstore. Turning to her, he said, "You must be new around here if you haven't heard of the work the government is doing. Otherwise, you'd know we're not very popular in Freedom."

"Why?" Janet asked curiously.

"The local people really don't want the project," he explained. With a grin he added, "Since your reputation is already damaged from riding through town with me, why don't you let me buy you a Coke?"

Janet glanced at the store, then ran a hand through her wind-tossed hair, and looked uncertainly at her sand-covered sandals.

"You look great," he assured her.

From the way he said it, she knew he meant it. She wasn't extremely susceptible to flattery, but it had been a long time since she had heard such sincere compliments and she found herself liking them—and Ron. In a subtle way he reminded her of Lars. "I'd love to have a soda," she smiled.

Inside the small drugstore, they gave their order to the girl at the counter and Janet sat down in a booth. The fountain section only had one booth and a counter with four stools; the rest of the room was given over to magazines and sundries. An adjoining door led to another room where small antiques were on sale.

Ron seated himself across from her. "I know you're not from here, so where is your home?" he asked.

"Indiana," she supplied before taking a sip of her drink.

"Do you work in the area?"

"I teach grade school in town," Janet told him.

"Did you go to college in Oklahoma?"

"No."

"Do you have relatives here?" he pursued.

He was obviously wondering what had brought

her to Oklahoma, especially to Freedom, but Janet did not enlighten him. She just shook her head silently. She didn't want to go into an explanation of the events that caused her to leave Indiana.

Ron looked faintly puzzled. "I hope you don't think I'm prying, but I'm surprised you came here. I mean, Freedom is a quaint little place, but it's hardly where most people start their careers."

Janet gave a cheerful laugh. "That's true," she agreed. "However, I don't intend to stay here indefinitely." As she spoke, she remembered Jason Stewart's words of last night. He had said he could have her fired and he didn't seem like a man to make idle threats. So perhaps her time in Freedom would be even shorter than she had anticipated. Would he really try to have her dismissed? she wondered, as she took a drink of her cherry Coke.

"You're not married, are you?" he asked.

The question did not surprise her. "No."

Ron smiled. "Good. I was hoping you weren't. Would you like to go out Saturday night?"

It was a question Janet had been expecting and she had already decided on an answer. Ron Leonard was an attractive man and it was certainly time she started dating again. "All right," she said softly.

"Pick you up at seven?" he asked.

"That would be fine." After she told him where she lived the conversation turned back to his work in western Oklahoma. They finished their Cokes and walked slowly back outside.

"Our work here—" Ron stopped in midsentence and raised his hand to someone across the street. As he motioned the person to come over, Janet glanced up disinterestedly. She stiffened at the sight of Jason Stewart crossing the street toward them.

"I've been meaning to talk to you," Ron greeted him. "We'll probably be going in on your land next week. I wanted to let you know and find out if there's any certain road you want us to use."

"No," Jason replied. "The same one you used last time is fine."

"Good. I have to go now," Ron said briskly. He turned to Janet. "Saturday, seven," he reminded her with a smile.

She nodded as he got into the truck and drove away. She was left standing on the sidewalk facing Jason.

"Well," he said with a slight lift of one eyebrow, "does he have a niece in your class also?"

"No, he doesn't," she said with artificial sweetness, "but I'm sure if he did, he would listen to any suggestions offered to him by the child's teacher."

"A reference to my own obstinence, Miss Matthews?" he drawled. "I still abide by my decision—I won't tolerate interference in family matters. However, I may have been a little unfair to you last night. Since you apparently intended no harm, I am willing to forget the matter. I will make no complaint to the board."

"You're too kind, Mr. Stewart," Janet said coolly and turned to leave.

CHAPTER 3

Saturday at seven Janet was dressed and waiting, confident that she looked good in her lilac knit sleeveless top with a tiny V notched into the scooped neckline. The matching skirt had provocative slits up each side which revealed her well-shaped legs when she walked. She had taken a long time to dress and she had fixed her copper-colored hair with great care. It was braided on the right side of her head with the braid caught in a little pinwheel over her ear. It was a sophisticated style she had seen in *Cosmopolitan*.

After putting on another dash of eye makeup, Janet surveyed herself critically in the dressing table mirror. Yes, she looked good. Her skin had taken on a bronze glow from her daily walks along the river, and a little blusher had heightened the two spots of color already present high on each cheek.

She gave her hair a final pat as a knock sounded on the door. Ron was right on time, she noted with satisfaction, as she moved to answer it. Pulling the door open, Janet greeted her date with a broad welcoming smile. It dimmed swiftly to a perplexed look.

Standing in the doorway, appearing windswept and casual in a blue shirt that was unbuttoned at the top, was Jason Stewart.

"May I help you?" she asked crisply.

"And you scolded me for not inviting you in when you dropped by my house," he remarked lightly. He held out his hands to present a bouquet of wildflowers to her.

She eyed them with a dampening look, but made no move to accept them.

"Don't worry, they're harmless," he assured her.

"Thank you, but I don't want your gifts," Janet said.

Disregarding her inhospitable words, he stepped past her into the house and strode toward the kitchen.

She followed, feeling a mixture of disbelief and annoyance. "What are you doing?" she demanded as he opened a cabinet.

"I'm going to put the flowers in water."

"Very thoughtful," she snapped. "That won't be necessary. I just want you to leave. I have a date and I don't want *you* here when he arrives."

"You don't have a date," he contradicted smoothly. As he talked, Jason took a tall tumbler from the cabinet and moved to the sink to fill it with water. After putting the flowers into the glass, he turned to face her. He looked disconcertingly tall and masculine in the tiny yellow kitchen. "Ron isn't coming," he told her quietly. "It's threatening to rain, so he and the crew are working until midnight to finish the core hole they're on and get the rig out of the river bottom while they still can."

"How do you know that?" she fired. Janet wasn't even sure she doubted the truth of what he said, but she did know it was irritating to receive such a message from Jason Stewart.

"I happened to be down where they're drilling and Ron asked me to call you and tell you he couldn't come. Since you're already dressed up," he surveyed her with a languid perusal that left her feeling more dressed down than up, "why don't—"

She cut through his suggestion with a sharp statement. "Why didn't you call and relay the message? Why are you here at all?"

He shrugged. "I was on my way into town anyway so I thought I'd drop by."

As he spoke another thought occurred to Janet. She straightend and looked at him coolly as he lounged against the Formica counter top. "When did Ron tell you he couldn't go tonight?"

"About four this afternoon," he replied, glancing indifferently around the clean kitchen. "Since you no longer have a date with him I thought you and I might do something."

"You thought wrong, Mr. Stewart," she said tartly. She looked from him to the door, a pointed invitation for him to depart.

"If you're hinting for me to leave, I will, but I think you're making a mistake. After all, Freedom *is* a rather boring town and I doubt you've had that much to do since school let out. You are already dressed to go somewhere and although I may not be the date intended," he said with a slow smile, "I do have the advantage of being available."

"Thank you for your invitation, but no thanks," Janet replied in clipped tones.

"Suit yourself. But you have put some time into getting ready so I figured you wanted to go out and enjoy yourself. Of course, if you insist on being stubborn . . . ," he ended with a shrug.

"I am *not* stubborn," Janet denied. Hearing her own words and seeing the smile of disbelief that crossed Jason's face, she felt a smile tremble on her own lips. Perhaps she was being hardheaded, she conceded. She *was* terribly bored and she realized she would be even more so after Jason left and she had the rest of the evening at her disposal.

"Of course you're not," he soothed. "So prove it by allowing me to take you out."

"You have a way of manipulating people with challenges, don't you?" she asked. But her good humor was coming to the fore. And more than that she had a curious desire to know what made Jason Stewart tick. She knew he really did want her to go. He was actually going to some trouble tonight to try to persuade her to spend the evening with him. A part of her was flattered at that thought. She nodded. "I'll go," she murmured.

As they started for his car, she wondered at herself. Why was she willing to be with someone she really didn't like rather than being alone? She doubted she would have a good time.

Janet was wrong; she enjoyed herself. Jason turned out to be an interesting conversationalist with a knowledge of a great many subjects. At least for this one night he seemed intent on being pleasant. They had a good dinner at a cozy supper club in Woodward, lingering over drinks afterward.

By the time he returned her to her house, Janet was in a good frame of mind and much more charitably disposed toward him. She invited him in and flipped on the television as he followed her into the house.

"Sit down," she directed as she gestured toward

the couch. "I'll get some chips and drinks and we can watch the late movie." She returned a few minutes later and seated herself beside him.

Janet's mind was never fully engaged with the movie in progress. She was too conscious of the man beside her, waiting for him to initiate something. She knew he would. There was only one light on. It gave a warm glow to the room and intensified the subtle sense of intimacy she felt. Then Jason moved closer, slipped a hand over her shoulder, and drew her nearer to him. With one easy movement he turned off the table light and bent to kiss her. It was the moment she had been expecting and when it happened, she felt both relief and a new tenseness. It had been a long time since a man had kissed her and she wanted him to go slowly and gently.

She didn't know if he sensed her feeling or if he was making a tentative test of her response, but he started carefully. The hard line of his lips barely touched her own soft lips. Then his tongue moved silkily, almost imperceptibly across her mouth until her lips parted pliantly under his. She felt a wave of anxiety roll off her and something stirred deep within, a hunger for more substantial contact with him than the tormentingly short caresses on her mouth. Janet raised her head to bring her mouth to his. He accepted the invitation with an embrace that pulled the breath from her body and left her yearning for more. Her earlier fears were all erased. She no longer anticipated what would happen next. She was content to drift with the tide, feeling safe in Jason's arms. It seemed unnecessary for either of them to think; at least she was not. A sixth sense seemed to be in control, one that knew unfailingly what to do next. She had only to enjoy.

She was doing more than that; she was positively reveling in the sure way he held her and the way his kisses sent a dizzying warmth spreading through her. She felt happy and blissfully limp. Whatever else Jason Stewart might be, she knew he was definitely experienced. Janet was no rag doll to melt in a man's arms. She had dated enough men to know how to handle herself, but he was arousing responses no man had elicited before. She was glad to give herself over to his direction, to savor his branding kisses while his hands roamed freely over her body.

She was vaguely conscious that he was sliding one hand up under her blouse, freeing her breasts of their confinement. Jason drew back slightly. Her lashes were closed and fanned out on her face, but she knew he was looking at her. A smile of sweet languidness curved her lips upward before she fluttered her lashes open. In the faint light from the window she beheld the startling blue of Jason's eyes. There was an expression in them she had never seen before, something curiously unreadable. The moment passed and she was lulled back into a state of mindlessness as Jason dropped snowflake soft kisses on her lips.

While his hands slowly learned her body, he began another exploration of her mouth—reaching deeper and with more passion. Responding to the excitement he aroused in her, Janet reached a hand up to pull him closer. Her fingers moved in a slow massage of the tender skin at the back of his neck. He gave a soft groan.

Janet's mind played small tricks on her as it ducked in and out of consciousness. Where his hands moved on her body she felt a reassuring heat, as if passion were flowing out through his fingertips and warming her with its intensity. Her senses were alive with his touch, and wrapped around her was the clean, masculine smell of him and the sound of his breathing in unison with hers. When he shifted slightly, she moved closer against him and opened her lips further to receive the darting lashes of his tongue.

If anyone had asked her at the moment where she was, she could only have answered that she was with Jason. For the present that was all that she really knew. While she was held tightly in his arms, her past seemed a faint shadow and the future remote. The whole lean length of his body arched closer to hers and she felt the unmistakable sign that his passion for her was as intense as hers for him.

"Janet," he whispered, "let me love you."

Yes, she wanted him to. She wanted this feeling to continue, to grow, and she knew Jason could make that happen.

"Let me, Janet," he murmured again. His mouth trailed a burning path of kisses over her ear before he began a sensuous exploration of it with his moist tongue, leaving her breathless and confused.

The cloud of passion lifted from her brain and reality edged in with his words. She was not the type of woman to be swept off her feet by a man of experience. She did want him, but only for now, only to fill a physical need. When the morning came, how would she feel about herself if she gave in to the desires of the moment? The answer to that question was clear.

"Don't," she whispered.

"Don't what?" Jason's voice was muffled against her throat as his mouth slid downward.

"Touch me."

"Janet," his words were soft and persuasive—like rain falling on dry sand, "don't stop me now. We both want this."

"No," she shook her head in denial.

"You're a woman, Janet, with a woman's needs. There's nothing wrong with wanting to be completely with a man."

She blinked her eyes open. Above her, only inches away, she saw Jason watching her. His eyes were smoky crystals of passion and his mouth was a sensuous line. If she let him continue, she knew she was lost. Mustering her resolution, she shook her head firmly. "It can't be like this, not for me."

He moved slowly away from her. In the sepia brown room she could not see his features clearly, but his voice bespoke his regret. "No, I guess it never could." Standing, he continued softly, "Sometimes I forget the line that separates the things I can have and the things I can't. Good night, Janet."

He had closed the door and was gone before she could speak. Janet stared after him for some minutes with her face cupped in her hands as she tried to sort through the events of the evening.

The most astounding thing, she considered with wonder, was that she had wanted him. She had not thought she would be so susceptible to any man, least of all Jason Stewart. All he could have felt for her was the desire of a man for a woman's body and her need for him had been just as primal. Why had she nearly surrendered to him? she puzzled. She had always felt that sex should come only when there was a very special emotion between a man and woman. She had never before considered going to bed with a man simply for a night's gratification.

She roused herself from her reflections to rise and walk to the bathroom. She had always been in control of her life, she reminded herself, as she pulled off her clothes and turned on the water in the tub. She was not going to lose that control because a man had temporarily upset her balance. Stepping into the bathtub, she stretched out with her eyes closed while it filled with water.

Visions of Jason floated across her mind. He was a mystery. At their first meeting, he had been inexcusably rude and when she had taken Susan home, he had certainly done nothing to endear himself to her. But she still had an undeniable physical attraction for him. In fact, after tonight, it was even stronger. He did have a way with women, she recalled with a smile.

But he wanted too much, she reminded herself sternly. Still . . . What had he meant by his parting remark? He had sounded regretful when he said he should know the difference in what he could and couldn't have. Surely he could have whatever he wanted.

Janet awoke by degrees the following morning. After rising and giving a cat stretch, she pulled on her robe and padded into the kitchen. In the act of taking a box of cereal from the cupboard, she caught a glimpse of the wildflowers Jason had brought last night.

She set the box down abruptly. It was poised precariously on the edge of the counter, but she was heedless of it for the moment. Her mind was occupied with the perplexing question of why Jason had brought her flowers. He was not the kind of man to do such a thing.

In fact, he was a person who seemed motivated by doing whatever was necessary to achieve his end. This morning Janet felt a faint hostility toward him which had not been present last night. Perhaps, she considered, she was being more objective now than she had been when he was present or fresh in her mind. The force of his presence and the physical enjoyment he had given her must have colored her thinking for a time, she thought dryly.

He had brought the flowers because he must have thought she would make a few chance-picked blossoms worth his time. As that thought crossed her mind, Janet picked up the bouquet and jammed it, petals down, into the wastebasket. She didn't want any reminders of last night.

A persistent patter called Janet back to the present. She looked out the gingham-curtained window to see great droplets of rain splattering against the pane. It was finally raining as Ron had feared it would.

She wondered briefly if Ron and the workmen had gotten the rig out of the river before the rain had started. Then she picked up the bowl and walked over to the round oak table, seating herself in a pattern-back chair. She turned her attention to her solitary meal, realizing regretfully that the bad weather would put an end to her hiking plans for the day. She hoped there was something good on television or that the rain would not last long.

By noon, neither of those events had occurred.

The sky was a watery leaden gray that held the promise of continued rain. The television offered only game shows and soap operas, neither of which appealed to Janet.

A sharp rap on the door brought her off the couch with an enthusiastic bound. If it was the Fuller brush man, she was going to invite him in and have him demonstrate every product he had—anything to alleviate her boredom. Pulling the door open, she saw a wet face smiling at her.

"Sorry about last night," Ron greeted her. He was standing in the deluge wearing a yellow vinyl slicker, with the hood pulled up.

"Come in," she said with a wide smile.

"No, I can't stay. I'm on my way back to Tulsa for a few days. I just wanted to stop by to apologize for last night. I guess Jason Stewart called to tell you I was tied up."

"He let me know," Janet said dryly.

"Good. Well, I'll be going."

"Wait!" Janet called as he turned.

He pivoted back and looked questioningly at her.

Confused, she groped for something to say. She really had no reason to detain Ron, but she was hungry for company. "Terrible weather, isn't it?" Before he had time to reply to her inane question she thought of a more inspired one. "I'm thinking of applying for a job elsewhere. Is Tulsa a good place to work?"

"Why, yes. It has a high per capita income and it's a pleasant city. If you'd like, I can give you the names of some of the area school systems."

"Oh yes! Come in and you can write them down for me while I fix you a cup of coffee."

"I'd like to, Janet, but I really have to get back to give a report of operations to my boss. He won't be there tomorrow so I have to prepare it before he leaves today."

"Oh." She could hear the dejection in her own voice.

Ron must have noted it too, but he put a different interpretation on it. "If you need the names now, get a pencil and paper and I'll give them to you. That way I won't have to come in and drip all over your carpet."

Janet nodded before turning and rushing into the kitchen to pick up a pencil with a dull point and tear off a piece of grocery sack. She returned to the living room and jotted down the names of the school systems he gave her.

"Thanks," she told him as she scribbled the last one on the brown paper.

"Sure," Ron replied, his mind moving on to something of greater interest. "I asked Jason to bring you some flowers from me but I don't suppose he thought of it."

Her mouth formed a small "o" of surprise. So the flowers hadn't been Jason's idea after all. She felt curiously deflated by that knowledge. Well, what difference did that make anyway, she rallied herself. Considering she had thrown them away, they couldn't have been that special to her.

"Did he bring them?" Ron pressed.

"Yes. Yes, he brought them," she murmured. "Thanks, they're beautiful." She thought of the flowers wilting in the wastebasket as she spoke the words, but gave no indication they did not occupy a place of honor in her house.

"Good." Ron grinned, standing in the drenching rain while water dripped off his nose. He huddled further back into the vinyl slicker. "Listen, I've really got to go. I'll call you when I get back."

"When do you think that will be?"

Ron looked gratified that she was so anxious to see him again. "In a week or so. It won't be very long," he assured her.

Janet nodded and then watched him run across the yard, making long-legged leaps over the puddles on the soupy lawn. He slid into his black and white truck, started the engine, and drove off down the street.

She sighed and closed the door. Well, there went her prospect for relief from some of her boredom. But at least now she had a definite task before her and she was going to begin her letters of application to Tulsa schools immediately. Jason's threat to have her fired had started her thinking about leaving anyway. Perhaps it was the best thing, she considered. Freedom had been a good place to ease herself through the first months of her loss, but it was time to move on.

Walking into her bedroom she pulled her portable typewriter from under the chenille-covered bed and lugged the machine into the kitchen. She spent the remainder of the day writing letters and typing them up.

The next day Janet ventured out into a rain so thick she thought fleetingly that it looked as though she could lean on it. The streets were empty. It was definitely not weather for strolling, but Janet wanted to mail her letters and she had no stamps. Several drenching minutes later she had posted the envelopes

"Now there's a man you should go after, hon," Bessie advised.

"I think he's taken," Rita observed dryly. "At least I saw him at a very fancy restaurant in Tulsa a couple of months back and he was with a striking blonde." Her eyes reassessed Janet and the look on her face implied that Janet came up lacking compared with the golden beauty.

Janet returned her look evenly, but made no reply.

"You're not saying anything," Rita prodded. "What do you think about Jason?"

"I don't know him very well, but I'm sure he's a nice person," Janet replied. He was not a man she cared to discuss with Rita. The knowledge he was squiring a woman around Tulsa was not surprising. After all, Lila had mentioned he was dating a woman from that city. Still, Rita's information made her perversely glad that nothing had happened between herself and Jason.

"You may be a little young for him," Rita noted with a candidness Janet found annoying. "I think he goes for sophisticated women."

"I'm twenty-six. I just happen to look younger." Janet added a sweet smile as an afterthought.

"I've always thought that Jason was a nice boy," Bessie interjected, "even if his mother was wild and ran off with that man. Besides," she addressed her daughter, "you haven't seen him enough to know what he's like."

"I know him," Rita argued. "He's been soured on people since the day his mother left and he hasn't changed a bit. He may be running around with knockouts, but I could tell by the offhand way he treated her that he was still the same."

biggest event of the year is the rodeo and it isn't until August. That could be a long dry spell."

"It doesn't look like a long dry spell," Janet laughed with a significant glance out the window toward the rain. "And besides, I've already met a man."

"Who?" Bessie demanded, her interest caught.

"His name is Ron Leonard and he works for the government. They're doing some investigations out here on a salt pollution problem. It's really quite interesting; he told me all about it."

"I know about the salt thing," Bessie said crisply, "that salt was there long before the white man came. I don't see no reason to go a-fooling with nature. Why, the Indians used to come from miles around to go to the big salt flats near Cherokee and they're going to ruin that too."

"Who is?" Rita asked.

"The government."

"Oh," Rita dismissed the subject. "I'm not interested in politics. I want to hear more about the men Janet is turning up under every stone. When I was a girl here, I used to go into Alva on Friday nights and drive around the college to meet guys."

"You didn't!" her mother denied in horror.

"I sure did, and Erica did too," she affirmed.

The name caught Janet's attention. "Erica?"

"Yeah, she was a girl in my class in school."

"Isn't she Jason Stewart's mother?" Janet pursued.

Rita looked at her in surprise, then blew a slow smoke ring, and dashed her cigarette out in an ashtray on the end table. "Is he a friend of yours?"

"I know him," Janet answered noncommittally.

dyed black hair and heavy makeup sauntered into the small living room, her shiny white jumpsuit looking oddly out of place in such sedate surroundings.

"Mother's been talking about you," she greeted Janet, "and I was telling her just this morning that I'd like to meet you. But the weather's been so bad we ain't been out any."

"I know, it's terrible," Janet agreed, accepting a glass of iced tea from Bessie as she talked, nodding her thanks. "but I was going stir crazy so I went out to mail some letters."

Rita settled herself onto a frayed brown couch and lit a cigarette. "I know what you mean about going stir crazy. I hadn't been back to Freedom for five years and I'd forgotten it was so damned dull."

Bessie bustled back into the room again and sat beside Rita, putting her own tea on a doily coaster atop a walnut end table. "That's exactly what I was a telling Janet just the other day. Young people aren't cut out for sitting around a dried-up town like this. Me, I like it, but I was born and raised here and I'm too old to go gadding about. But Janet here, I don't know how she's going to pass the summer." Bessie made a clucking nose and shook her gray head in bemusement.

Rita crossed her legs, the fabric of the jumpsuit catching in the light of a lamp and shimmering as it did so, "Mother's right. You'll go stark raving mad sitting in that little house all summer."

It was an assessment that Janet was inclined to agree with, but she noted fairly, "I wasn't exactly used to a busy social life in Indiana either."

"No, but there were surely men there," Rita pointed out. "where are you going to meet men here? The

and started back to her house, walking slowly in the downpour. She was already soaked, she reasoned, and there was no reason to hurry back to her house.

"Janet!" a voice shouted.

She looked up to see Bessie standing on her porch and motioning her toward the house. Splashing up the sidewalk, Janet greeted the older woman cheerfully. "Hi, Bessie. How are you enjoying being housebound?" she asked, hovering under the short roof of the porch.

"It doesn't bother me none," the old lady informed her matter-of-factly, "but it's about to drive my daughter crazy. Come on in and meet her; she'll be glad for the company."

"Are you sure I should? My clothes are dripping wet," Janet made a token protest even as she started in the door.

"It won't hurt this old rug any," Bessie assured her. "I'm going to have it taken up and new carpet put down anyway. Here, give me your coat."

Janet slipped out of her hooded jacket and handed it to Bessie.

"I'll just hang this up and tell Rita you're here," the old woman said, walking toward the kitchen with the garment sprinkling across the floor. "Rita, we've got company. It's that schoolteacher I was a telling you about." She turned back to Janet. "You just sit down, hon. Rita'll be here in a minute."

Janet sat on an overstuffed orange chair and looked around at the numerous photos of grandchildren and great-grandchildren lining the built-in bookcases and spilling over to the top of the television.

A moment later a woman in her middle fifties with

Janet thought they had talked about this particular man long enough. "So, you say you're getting new carpet?" She attempted to change the subject with a question to Bessie.

"Hey," Rita laughed, taking another long cigarette from her cigarette case and lighting it with a dramatic flick of a lighter. "You're avoiding the discussion of Jason. How did you meet him anyway? I didn't think he ventured off that *Giant*-style ranch except to go to the country club in Enid or dining in Wichita or Tulsa. I sure didn't think he hung around Freedom meeting the local teachers."

"His niece is in my class," Janet replied, using her words sparingly. She felt no desire to further explain her relationship with Jason to this woman.

"Niece?" Rita repeated. "What's this?"

"You remember," her mother supplied, "when Erica ran off, she took one of the two boys with her. He was killed in a car accident a few months back. Jason took his daughter to raise."

"Jason must make a hell of a father figure," Rita noted sarcastically.

Bessie turned to Janet. "Don't pay any attention to her, hon. He's always been friendly to me, even brought me home from the grocery store one day when I had a load too big to carry. He may be a little high-handed in some of his ways, but I'm sure the right woman could settle him down."

"That'd be like taming a Mexican fighting bull to ride," Rita sneered. "It may be possible, but I wouldn't want to be the one to try it. Stick with this other fellow, Janet. Mother just doesn't like him because he's with the government and she's still mad about the time they audited her tax return back in the fifties. Besides, she doesn't trust any man who isn't homegrown."

The discussion turned to less personal channels for a time before Janet finally rose to leave. "I have to go," she said as she put her glass down on a coaster. "Thanks for the tea, Bessie. I'm glad to have met you, Rita," she said to the other woman. The social amenities had to be observed, she thought with wry humor, even when they were meaningless.

Over Bessie's protests, Janet pulled her coat on and walked back out into the vertical flood, oblivious to the rain as she plodded back to her empty house.

CHAPTER 4

The following day the rain continued unabated as Janet sat curled up at one end of the red and blue sofa reading a romantic novel. Shifting restlessly, she laid the book aside and pulled back the blue serge curtains to look out the window. There she saw a miracle she had not witnessed for what seemed like weeks. The sun was making a valiant attempt to peek through the clouds and, best of all, the rain had stopped.

She put the book completely from her mind as she bounced off the couch and walked to the front door. Throwing it open, she breathed in the fresh scent of the day and looked thankfully toward the sky. She didn't think she could have stood another day boxed up in the house alone. Finally, she thought, a broad smile crossing her face, she would be able to go out and stretch her legs.

But where? The river would be swiftly flowing and extremely treacherous. Freedom itself was not large enough for her to spend more than ten minutes walking through before she had covered the whole of the town. She could visit someone, she considered, but there was only Bessie since Lila was out of the state for the summer. And Janet didn't want to go back to

Bessie's house until the black car in front of her house—indicating that Rita was still there—was gone. Janet had no desire to see Rita again.

She made another sweeping look across the clearing sky and then started in surprise at seeing someone standing not two feet away from her. She had been so intent on her thoughts she had not heard anyone approach.

"Hi," Susan greeted her with a bashful grin, "I hope I didn't scare you."

"Susan," she recovered herself, "what a surprise. What are you doing in town?"

"Uncle Jason thought the rain would clear around noon and he was right. Since I've been in the house for the last three days he promised to bring me into town and let me pick up a friend to take back out to the ranch."

"How nice."

"Yes," Susan agreed. "Will you come?"

Janet looked at the little redheaded girl in confusion. "What did you say?"

"Will you come to the ranch with me?" Susan repeated, shifting her weight on the top step and casting her eyes downward uncomfortably.

"I don't think—" Janet broke off uncertainly. Perhaps, she considered, Susan didn't know anyone else well enough to ask them. After all, she was a very retiring little girl and she had not fit in with any of the already established cliques when she had transferred to the school in midsemester. If Susan had no one else to ask, then Janet would not want to refuse her. Still, she didn't want to spend a day in the same house with Jason Stewart. Over the last few days she had come to the conclusion the less she saw of him the better it would be. It did not seem like a relationship that could ever go anywhere.

Janet's silence had the effect on Susan of a direct refusal. "Are you busy, is that why you can't go?" she mumbled, looking crestfallen as she kicked gently at a puddle on the top step.

"No, it's not that exactly. Well . . ." Janet wasn't sure how to proceed. It was too wet for them to do anything outside. But how could she tell Susan that she wouldn't come because there was friction between herself and Jason and that she didn't want to be in the house with him? She phrased her reply carefully. "Susan, I don't think your uncle would want me to visit. It might disturb him if he has things to do."

The little girl looked up with a tremulous smile. "Oh, he said I could invite anyone I wanted to. Actually," she continued with scrupulous honesty, "I went to Mary Louise's house first but nobody was home, and I couldn't think of anyone else I wanted to invite besides you. Will you come?" she reverted to the original question.

"I'm sorry, dear."

Susan turned away quickly but not before Janet caught the gleam of a tear in her eye. Damn Jason Stewart. She wasn't going to let him interfere with any enjoyment she could give this child.

"I'd be glad to come, Susan. Just let me change my clothes." The little girl's happy expression was the only reward she needed.

Five minutes later Janet was dressed in straight-legged jeans and a delicate pink camisole blouse. Her cinnamon-colored hair was caught back in a carefree ponytail and tied with a pink satin ribbon. Walking beside Susan toward the tiny downtown, she stepped jauntily, determined to make a pleasant day of it for both of them.

They reached a new-looking blue and white pickup parked in front of the hardware store. Susan opened the door and stood aside for Janet to slide in.

Janet peered inside at the tall man seated there. His head rested comfortably against the back of the seat, his gray felt hat was tilted at a casual angle on his head, and his eyes were closed. What did Susan mean by asking her to sit in the middle anyway? She didn't want to be so near Jason on the long drive to the ranch.

While she hesitated at the door of the truck, he slowly opened his cobalt eyes. A smile that conveyed a mixture of scorn and amusement crept across his sun-bronzed face. "So, you're the little friend Susan is bringing home for the day?"

"She invited me, yes," Janet responded aloofly.

"Go ahead and get in," Susan prompted, giving Janet a gentle push from behind.

Janet turned to the little girl, "I'd rather you rode in the middle."

"I don't want to," Susan retorted stubbornly. "I won't!" she added emphatically.

Jason's sardonic voice broke into the disagreement. "Are you two going to stand there and fight like a couple of kids or will *one* of you play the part of an adult and get in the truck?"

Janet gave a sigh of exasperation and slipped into the vehicle. It was plain Susan was not going to do so and Jason was right; it was a foolish thing to argue over.

"Oh," Susan said, still standing outside the vehicle. "I just remembered something I wanted to buy. You two wait here."

Janet moved from the middle back toward the door.

He laughed. "Don't be shy. It's obvious Cupid is taking the form of a bratty little girl these days."

"So I've noticed, but there's no need to encourage her," she responded dampeningly. She looked up to see Jason studying her figure with unconcealed appreciation.

"For such a young-looking little thing you seem to have all the right equipment," he grinned as he noted her look.

"This has all the makings of a bad trip," Janet returned. "I believe I'll stay at home. I don't think I am up to a full day of your remarks."

Jason unfurled a long arm across to her and gripped her wrist, imprisoning the soft flesh of it in his hard hand. "Oh no, you don't. I'm not going to have a bawling kid left on my hands when Susan comes back and finds you gone. You needn't worry about being forced to sit and listen to me. The purpose of having her bring someone to the ranch is so she will be out of my way while I'm entertaining a friend of my own." He regarded Janet with cynical humor. "It will all seem funnier to you later," he assured her.

The door behind Janet opened suddenly and only Jason's firm grip on her wrist kept her from sliding out. Susan crowded up into the seat. Janet moved back to the center of the bench seat. She was overreacting, she considered, as Jason started the engine and drove out of town down the long, black ribbon of road leading to the huge Stewart ranch. After all, she was only going to be in Jason's house a few hours. He had already assured her he would be busy so she wouldn't have to see much of him. More importantly, she didn't want to disappoint Susan.

Janet was brought out of her reflections as she felt Susan nudge closer to her, forcing her to shift slightly closer to Jason. A moment later Susan encroached again. Janet looked around the little girl to the widening space between the child and the door of the truck.

"You're crowding me, move back over," she directed firmly.

Susan pretended not to hear, flipping on the radio and adjusting the volume up loud as she squirmed nearer, forcing Janet even closer against Jason. Janet's hips were touching his as they sped down the road and the closeness brought to mind her last encounter with him. An unexpected thrill coursed through her at the memory. She was brought back to reality when Susan edged closer. Janet reached over and turned off the radio. "Young lady, move back to your side or I will have your uncle turn around and take me back to town."

Susan obeyed, silently sliding back to her place by the door and leaving Janet free to return to the center. As she did so, she looked at the little girl's averted face. Susan was feigning an interest out the window, but Janet could see that her cheeks were flushed and she knew Susan was embarrassed. Looking toward Jason, she saw he was also aware of his niece's feeling.

His expression was indifferent. "Leave her alone," he advised in a low voice.

Janet gave another uncertain glance at Susan and

decided Jason was right, at least for the present. She settled back uncomfortably and rode in silence until Jason smoothly maneuvered the truck off the highway and onto the wide road that led toward the ranch house. He avoided with precision the newly created chuckholes.

Susan opened the door almost before the vehicle had stopped moving. Janet watched the child run around the side of the house but she did not pursue. Instead, she walked toward the Spanish-style house and stopped at the door to wait for Jason to reach it at a more leisurely pace. A moment later he put a hand around her and opened it.

"Come in," he invited. "I hate to keep guests standing on the doorstep."

Janet ignored his sarcastic reference to her other visit and asked abruptly. "Where did Susan go?"

"She probably remembered something she wanted to do at the stables. Maybe," he confided with a wicked grin, "she wanted to give us some more time alone. Unfortunately," he continued, ushering Janet into the modern living room and closing the door. "I'm afraid that won't be possible. The car I hear pulling into the driveway is the company I am expecting."

A minute later a knock sounded at the door and Jason strode across the room and swung it open. A tall blond woman walked into the living room. Janet's eyes traveled from the long, shapely legs that carried her into the house, to her curvaceous body, and halted at her perfect face. It was sensual and stunning, framed by flowing silky hair.

"Darling," the woman greeted Jason, oblivious to

Janet as she nuzzled up to him and turned her lips upward to be kissed.

"Not yet, Georgia," he drawled, pulling away from her. "We have company." As the woman turned slowly toward her, Janet saw her green cat eyes were a perfect almond shape in a flawless oval face.

"This is Janet Matthews," Jason introduced her. "She is a friend of Susan's. Miss Matthews," he continued with mock formality, "meet Georgia."

The blonde's delicately arched brows lifted. "I'd have thought Susan would bring home friends her own age," she cooed as her arm possessively encircled his lean waist. She smoothed his plaid cotton shirt with a long, red fingernail before turning back to face him. She reached a slender hand up to Jason's neck and brought his head down to hers. "Umm, good," Georgia murmured as her lips fell back from his. "We can go somewhere that we won't be disturbed, can't we?"

"Don't mind me," Janet interrupted. Georgia was obviously putting on this show for her benefit. "You two enjoy yourselves. I'll go find Susan." Janet walked through the modern red and white kitchen and out the back door.

Outside, Susan was sitting on a damp step at the edge of a wide semicircular patio overlooking a swimming pool. She looked up as Janet sat down beside her, then looked away again. Janet followed the child's gaze off into the distance where a rolling line of hills disappeared into the blue-gray horizon. There was a wistful softness on Susan's face that prevented Janet from interrupting her thoughts by speaking.

The little girl broke the silence with a simple statement. "So she came."

Her words were eloquent with defeat. Janet looked at her curiously and scattered pieces of a jigsaw puzzle began to come together, taking shape into a picture that was both logical and disturbing. Susan, she suddenly realized, had been attempting to spark a romance between herself and Jason in the hope of turning his interest away from Georgia.

"Don't you like her?" Janet asked.

Susan lifted her shoulders and let them fall in an attempt at indifference that failed miserably. It had been an unnecessary question anyway. It was apparent she did not.

"Where do your parents live?" Susan asked unexpectedly.

"They're dead," Janet replied simply.

"Mine are too."

"Yes, I know."

"When it first happened," Susan continued, "I just wanted to run away."

Janet turned her gaze back to the shimmering pool and listened to Susan speak. It was as if someone else was telling of how she had felt at the time of her own parents' deaths and the death of Lars.

"I don't think it's something you can run away from," Janet said, speaking into the distance. Her words were directed to the far-reaching hills and the prairie sky as well as to the little girl beside her.

"You did," Susan objected, bringing Janet back to reality with a jolt.

"Not really—" Janet began and stopped. That was a lie, to herself as well as to Susan. She *had* run away. She had been unable to face the world she had known when it had changed without warning and she had fled.

"Perhaps you're right," she admitted slowly, pulling her eyes back to her companion. "I did. But it was probably the wrong thing to do. I think I should have stayed in Indiana and tried to sort out my feelings there instead of leaving and starting over here."

"Do you think I should have stayed in New Jersey?"

Janet looked down at the serious little face upturned to her. "It's not the same for you. You have to live with someone who can support you. You need to be with someone who'll care for you."

Susan considered that statement gravely, then nodded her head, her red pigtails bouncing up and down with the movement. "Yes," she agreed and continued with a startling change of subject. "Come on down and see the pool," she cried as she raced down the terrace steps. She stopped at the bottom to wait as Janet rose and followed.

"Want to swim? The sun's out now and the water isn't cold," she announced, bending by the pool to scoop up a handful of water. She let it trickle down through her small fingers onto the concrete.

"I don't have a suit," Janet objected.

"There's one in the bathhouse." Susan pointed toward a modern-looking building with blue and white striped sailcloth awnings. "We have one that fits all sizes. I'm sure you can wear it. Georgia does," she added. "I don't like to swim by myself, but no one ever goes with me. Georgia swims with Jason sometimes. One night I looked out my bedroom window and they were—"

"Susan!" Janet interrupted severely, "I am not interested in hearing about your uncle's private affairs and I am sure he would not want you telling them to me." She softened her tone as an expression of hurt pride crossed the child's face. "Let's change and we'll swim for a while."

Susan led her to the bathhouse and flipped on a light switch. The illumination revealed a room with slatted wooden floors over a concrete slab and three individual curtained dressing rooms. The little girl picked up a canary yellow suit from a shelf beside a large stack of towels.

"I'll change in the middle one," she said, walking toward the dressing room. "You can wear that black suit on the shelf."

Janet took the one Susan indicated and stepped into a corner dressing room. She began to shed her camisole top and tight-fitting jeans. A few moments later she stood in a revealing black suit that molded to her body, accentuating every curve. Janet surveyed her flat stomach and small but firmly rounded bust hesitantly. It *was* a terribly revealing suit and the center plunge went nearly to her navel with only the tiniest little tie at the bosom making even a feeble attempt at modesty. Well, she considered, it was the only suit available so she had no choice but to wear it.

Stepping out of the bathhouse into the sunshine, Janet walked over to the pool. She took a deep breath before plunging into the water in a graceful dive. She smelled the tangy chlorine just before she touched the surface of the smooth water. Gliding through the cool liquid across the narrow width of the pool, she emerged breathless on the other side. She flipped the wet hair back from her face with a quick toss of her head. The pink ribbon that had held her ponytail in place slipped from her hair, letting the escaped strands brush against her shoulder.

"Get in," she shouted to Susan who hovered near the edge of the pool, her arms wrapped tightly around her body.

"It's too cold!" Susan objected, a tentative toe delicately testing the water.

"It was your idea to come swimming," Janet reminded her with a laugh before making a surface dive back into the tranquil water and moving through the noiseless world with the easy grace of a water nymph.

It was a full hour later before Janet pulled herself from the water, shivering as the cold air hit her. She was exhausted. After coaxing Susan into the water the two of them had raced each other back and forth across the pool until they were breathless. Then they had tossed a beach ball back and forth until it had glanced off the edge of the pool so hard that it popped with the force. Undaunted, they had turned their energy to taking turns diving off the board.

"No more," Janet laughed, panting from exertion as she pulled herself up at the edge of the pool.

Susan emerged from the water beside her and scampered into the bathhouse. She returned a minute later with two large blue towels and handed one to Janet before wrapping the other one around herself. Janet huddled inside the towel on the concrete near the pool.

"See that building over there," Susan pointed a dripping index finger off into the distance.

Janet's eyes searched the red hills until the gentle ridges faded away into the distant buttes. "No."

"Right there," Susan nodded her head, "just to the right of that big mesquite and beyond that salt cedar."

"I don't know one from the other," Janet admitted with a laugh. "But I think I can see a little square building quite a way from here. It's about the same color as the orangish earth around it. Is that what you're talking about?"

"Yes. That was the original cabin the Stewarts lived in when they homesteaded the land. This land was in the Cherokee Outlet and it was part of the Land Rush of 1893," Susan informed her knowledgeably. "At least that's what our foreman, Hank, says," she added fairly. "That happened before I came from New Jersey."

Janet suppressed a smile and ran a hand through her hair, the red sheen of it bronze now with dampness. "I'm sure he's right."

"Yes. He said life was very hard on the grassland then. It was harder before they built the cabin because up until then they lived in a sod house. This house," she motioned back to the large, Spanish-style house behind them, "wasn't built until a few years ago. That's when they found oil on the land. That plus the cattle—"

"Perhaps," a male voice interrupted from above them, "Miss Matthews is not interested in your family history."

Janet glanced up to see Jason staring down at her. His cool blue eyes made a dispassionate appraisal of her towel-wrapped body before he lowered his tall frame onto the concrete beside her. Janet pulled her knees up to her chest, wrapping her arms protectively about them.

"Cold?" he asked with false concern.

"I'm fine, thank you. Don't you have company?" Janet asked sweetly.

"Yes," he answered, while his eyes rested on her smooth, browned legs, "but she's making a phone call right now."

"Janet," Susan interjected excitedly, "show Uncle Jason how you swan dive." Addressing herself to Jason, Susan continued, "This is really something! Just watch. Go ahead," she directed Janet.

"I don't want to go back into the cold water," Janet demurred.

"Please," Susan urged, "just one."

"I think," Jason said with an assessing look at Janet's towel-clad torso, "that Miss Matthews is reluctant to demonstrate her expertise while I'm here. You needn't worry about showing your figure to me, Miss Matthews," he assured her with an indolent smile, "I've seen women's bodies before. At swimming pools, I mean."

"I am sure you have," she agreed, a note of pleasantness was deliberately infused into her voice. Had Susan not been present, she would have made a far different response.

"Please," Susan intervened again, "show us your swan dive."

There were other things Janet would rather have done than demonstrate her mediocre dive for Jason in a suit that left little to the imagination, but Susan was insistent. Standing, she let the towel fall to the ground as she walked to the diving board and climbed the ladder. She paused at the top before walking the length in measured steps, bouncing at the end of the board and arching up into the air to execute the graceful dive. She plunged into the chilly water below and surfaced a moment later. Swimming to the edge of the pool, she pulled herself out with an easy movement, then walked back to the pair and bent to pick up her towel again.

"Isn't she terrific? Have you ever seen anything like that?" Susan demanded of her uncle.

"Admirable," he murmured in agreement. But when Janet flicked a glance at him, she knew it was not her diving form about which he was commenting.

CHAPTER 5

After a light lunch, Janet and Susan spent three hours in the little girl's room, putting together a complex puzzle of a black widow spider in a finely-wrought web. Sitting cross-legged on the floor of the bedroom, Janet raked her fingers through the pieces left in the pile, looking for something with a touch of red on it.

"I wish she hadn't come," Susan said suddenly, breaking the companionable silence in a terse voice.

Janet didn't have to ask who; she knew. But she was determined not to give Susan any reason to dwell on Georgia's visit so she said nothing. Susan averted her eyes downward and jammed a piece into the puzzle. It obviously did not fit into the slot she had forced it into. Janet began to pry the misplaced piece out of the spider's fuzzy leg, keeping her head bowed as she worked.

"She usually stays all night," Susan revealed in a melancholy voice.

Janet glanced at her watch. It was time she was going. If for no other reason than because Susan seemed on the verge of revealing a great deal more about Jason's affairs than she wanted to know. "I really should be leaving; I wonder if Rosa or Hank could take me back to town."

"Uncle Jason will take you," Susan offered readily.

"No," Janet said in a gentle but firm voice. "I don't want to bother him."

"Then I'll go ask Hank," she conceded reluctantly.

Janet smiled after the child as she left the room. It was plain Susan still wanted her uncle to spend his time with Janet. Her matchmaking stratagems were artless and transparent, but at least she had persistence. A moment later she heard Susan in the hall, talking to Jason.

"Janet wants to go home."

"I'll take her," Jason answered.

"That's what I told her but she said to have Hank do it," Susan reported.

His voice was louder when he spoke again and Janet suspected the added volume was for her benefit. "Miss Matthews doesn't order my hired help around in my home. Tell her I'm ready to leave right now."

The annoyance in Jason's voice and the message he conveyed irritated Janet, but she listened calmly when Susan returned with an account of her uncle's words.

"I had a nice day. Thank you for inviting me."

Susan's mouth creased into a toothy grin and she gave Janet an impulsive hug before turning and scurrying out of the room with a speed that indicated shyness over her display of affection.

Janet smiled after her and walked to the front

door, stepping out into the late afternoon. The brilliant gold of the approaching sunset had painted the earth and sky a surrealistic metallic color. She was fleetingly appreciative of it as she started toward the blue and white truck.

"We'll take the car," Jason said behind her. He walked to a silver Mercedes and held the passenger door open for her.

She settled back comfortably as they started the long trip into town. The interior of the expensive car, with its maroon leather seats, fleece floor mats, and walnut trim, was the picture of understated elegance. Jason appeared as at ease in it as he had been in his pickup. But then, Janet realized, he was a man who would be at home in any world.

Until now she had thought of him only as a rancher. Wearing jeans fitted to his narrow hips and a stetson hat planted on his head, that was what he had seemed. But this was altogether a different image. Now he wore a beige linen shirt and brown slacks fitted to his long legs with a tailor's precision. He could be a company executive or a lawyer. He looked the part of the shrewd and successful businessman. Of course, she considered, he must be just that to manage such a vast ranch.

Yes, he was prosperous in his business. He had a flint edge that must stand him in good stead in that arena. What about his more personal associations? Were they successful? It was obvious he did not limit himself to one woman. Did he find happiness with the many he must date?

"What have you decided about me?" Jason demanded, never taking his eyes from the road.

"You don't miss anything, do you?" She answered his question with another one.

"Very damn little," he replied flatly. "I wouldn't be where I am today if I didn't know what people around me were thinking."

"I love a modest man," she murmured.

"Honesty is a better route than deceptive humility," Jason replied calmly.

"Are you always honest?" she asked with a glance at him. "Somehow I didn't picture you telling Georgia about the evening you and I spent together less than two weeks ago."

"Are your feathers ruffled about that?" he asked with a lopsided grin.

"Why should they be?" she countered.

"Well, we did have a reasonably good time until . . . , shall I say, the end of the date. Are you annoyed I didn't call back? If you'd like, we can try it again. Say this Saturday?"

Janet looked at him in disbelief. "Are you serious? You have a woman waiting for you back at your ranch and you're trying to make a date with me? I call that rather insulting to both of us."

"Careful planning is all," he said modestly. "Georgia won't be here this Saturday and you will."

"Yes, I will," she snapped, "but not for you."

Jason shrugged as he pulled up in front of her house. "Suit yourself."

"I'm glad you are not utterly dejected by my refusal," Janet said with irony lacing her words.

"Man's got to be realistic," he observed casually.

Janet opened the door and stepped out. "Thank you for bringing me home. Good-bye," she said with cool crispness. He was smiling when he drove away and the remembrance of that expression was particularly irritating to Janet. He had a lot of nerve to ask her out under these circumstances.

Inside the house she put Jason firmly from her mind as she fixed a light supper and ate it in front of the television. Then she settled down with a book she had picked up at the library. By degrees, she became involved in the murder mystery she was reading. Forgetting time, she was conscious only of the prickling sense of anticipation the book aroused.

She was almost to the end and the suspense was building rapidly when a sharp knock on the door caused her to jump. Her nerves were on edge and she was alert as she stood apprehensively. The clock on the wall showed it was midnight. Who would be calling at that hour? That was when old Mrs. Winters in the second chapter had been murdered. It had been midnight and she had just put her cat out.

Another furious burst of knocks sounded on the wooden door.

"Who is it?" she called, remembering how Mrs. Winter had edged toward her kitchen for her sharp butcher knife.

"Jason," he barked, "let me in, it's urgent."

She relaxed and moved quickly to the door to swing it open. Jason stood outlined in the darkness, his hair tousled by the night wind.

"Do you know where Susan is?" he demanded in a hard voice without preliminary exchange of pleasantries.

"What?" she asked in confusion.

"My niece is gone. Do you have any idea where?"

"I don't know," Janet said, running a hand

through her hair in agitation. "The last time I saw her was before you brought me home."

"She's been gone since nine," he said tersely.

"That's nearly three hours!" Janet cried in alarm.

"Yes, I've notified the authorities and they're looking. I'm checking places I thought she might have gone. I guess I'd better keep looking," he said as he turned to leave.

"Wait!" she called. "I'll go with you."

"There's no need for that."

"But I want to and I'd be too worried to sleep anyway."

"All right," he agreed. "I'll wait while you put something on."

Janet turned and walked into her bedroom and closed the door. For the first time since Jason's arrival, she was conscious of her attire. The white gown with tiny smocking around the rounded neckline revealed a clear view of her body beneath. Only a pair of bikini panties saved her from being totally nude under the semisheer gown.

She pulled the nightgown over her head and donned a pair of black gabardine slacks before snapping on a bra and slipping a black and tan T-shirt over her head. Then she drew a heavy wool sweater from the oak dresser and stepped back into the living room.

Jason was standing over the television looking at the picture atop it. It was one taken the day after Lars had proposed to her, a studio portrait of her with Lars and her parents.

"These your parents?" he asked, pointing to the couple seated in front of her and Lars.

"Yes."

"Who's the guy? Brother?"

"A friend," she said noncommitally.

"Do they live near here?"

"No, they don't," she replied simply, and forestalled any further questions by opening the door and stepping outside.

Inside the car, Jason started the motor and drove toward the downtown section of Freedom. He traversed Main Street slowly, looking out the window carefully in each direction. When he reached the end, he turned to Janet. "When you were with her today, did you say anything to upset her? he asked bluntly.

"Of course not," she responded. She stopped herself from adding more when a glance at him revealed lines of worry etched in his face. This was not the time to be sensitive about her feelings.

"Where do you think Susan might have gone?" he asked.

Janet considered the things she and Susan had discussed that day at the ranch—during their swim and afterward when they had been working on the jigsaw puzzle. Jumbled snatches of their conversations whirled through her head. "We talked about her parents," Janet said slowly, struggling to remember the rest of the conversation.

"What did she say about them?" he fired at her.

"She said perhaps she shouldn't have left New Jersey—that it might have been running away for her not to have stayed there and faced the reality of their deaths. Maybe," Janet suggested with a growing sense of unease," she's going to try to go back to New Jersey."

"How would she do that?"

"There's the bus out of Alva," she said reluctantly.

"That's twenty miles from Freedom. I don't know how she could have made it from the ranch to here, let alone getting any farther."

"She might have hitchhiked," Janet offered.

The thought of a small child out on a dark highway by herself sent a cold shiver up her spine. She glanced at Jason and could see, from the faint light from the dashboard of the car, that his face was set in a hard line. He said nothing, but he turned the car toward Alva and began the drive to the bus station, going slowly and watching the sides of the road as he drove.

Four hours later Jason stopped the car in front of her stucco house and leaned his head wearily against the steering wheel.

"Well," Janet said unnecessarily, "we've been everywhere. She wasn't at the bus station in Alva or Enid and we've notified the sheriffs in Woods and Woodward counties. The state police are looking for her. There's nothing else we can do."

He did not reply. He was still slumped against the wheel. "Why don't you come in and have something to drink?" Janet suggested.

Jason responded like a robot, getting out of the car and walking mechanically up to the door of the house, without looking back at her. Janet followed him up the walk and stepped past him to open the door.

Inside the house, Janet flipped the light switch on. Jason sat down in the living room while she continued into the kitchen and put some water on to boil. As she took the instant coffee out of the cabinet, her mind wandered back to the thought that had been haunting her throughout the whole search. Why had Susan run away? The idea that she might have been kidnapped had been quickly dispelled when Jason had informed her Susan's small suitcase was missing. What would prompt a seven-year-old girl to brave the dangers of the dark and unknown to escape from her present predicament? She must have been miserable indeed to have done such a thing.

Janet stared out into the darkness through the window as she turned her mind to thoughts of Jason. What was his real reaction to Susan's flight? He was concerned, naturally, but was it any more so than any adult would have been over the disappearance of a child, even one that was not related? She was unable to answer those questions and the fact that she could not, upset her. It was possible, she thought, that the solution to the question of Jason's feelings toward Susan were deeply bound to the reason she had left. Perhaps they were also responsible for the painful shyness Susan displayed at school. Did Susan think her uncle disliked her?

"The water is boiling," Jason said beside her.

She started at the sound of his voice. "Oh. Oh, yes." She reached to take the kettle off the stove, but he stopped her.

"I don't care for any coffee and I think you need sleep more than you need a stimulant. Why don't you go to bed? I'll go on back to the ranch."

She heard the weariness in his voice and saw the slump of his shoulders. "That would be pointless. You can call the house and tell Rosa you're here. It will save you the long drive out there and you'll be in town if the police call. You can sleep on the couch."

He nodded in reply as she turned off the stove. Then she walked into the bedroom and stretched herself across the bed, disregarding the scratchy feel of the chenille spread on her face. She hadn't the energy to crawl under the covers.

Even her concern for Susan was overshadowed by the engulfing weariness of her own body and she ebbed into a sleep that hovered between slumber and a kind of drugged consciousness. People began to walk through her mind.

She was back in Indiana. She had just returned from a week of student teaching in tiny Shoals, Indiana, and she was so glad to be back. She ran into the house calling for her mother. Her mother wasn't in the kitchen but Janet could smell the spicy aroma of an apple pie. Her father wasn't in the den and the television wasn't on even though it was time for his favorite show. Lars wasn't there either, studying in the little corner desk in the living room where he usually sat. Where was everyone?

She looked through the house, running up the stairs, anxious to share the news of her week with them.

She knocked on the door of Lar's room. No answer. She opened the door slightly. He was lying in bed, his eyes closed. Smiling to herself she drew the door closed and hurried on down to her parents' room. They too were in bed, lying side by side, faint and peaceful smiles on their faces. She approached them in slow motion, bending to kiss her mother's cheek. It was like wax. Janet drew back and looked in disbelief. The face before her was cold and lifeless.

She ran around to the other side of the bed. Her father was dead too.

Somewhere in the distance she heard screams. She was standing over her parents' bed staring quietly down at them but somewhere someone was screaming.

Janet was jerked out of her dream by rough hands dragging her off the bed. She blinked at the man in front of her. Her gaze focused slowly on a tall man with wind-whipped brown hair. Where had she seen such blue eyes before? She didn't think she ever had. At least not any that showed the concern these did. She had seen some like them—blue, yes, but they had always been cold and forbidding.

"Are you all right?" he demanded, giving her a sharp shake.

"Oh," her mind snapped back into focus. "Yes. Yes, I'm fine."

"You were screaming bloody murder."

She drew back from him. "Was I?" she asked vaguely, "I must have been having a nightmare."

Jason looked at her closely and then dropped his arms from hers. "It's seven in the morning. I just called the ranch. No sign of Susan."

"Oh." Janet's back ached from last night's long ride and the uncomfortable position she had slept in. Added to that, her head was beginning to pound from lack of sleep and worry. Putting a hand to her forehead she rubbed across it as she rose.

"Do you feel okay?" he fired.

The tone of his voice struck a very raw nerve. "What do you care how I feel? The only reason you're worried about Susan is because it wouldn't look good to people if the great Jason Stewart's niece was killed trying to run away from him. You don't care a thing about her."

His gaze was level and unemotional. "It doesn't matter what my feelings toward her are. She is my responsibility and I'm going to find her."

Janet rubbed a hand across her eyes again and pushed back the hair tumbling into her face. "I'm sorry," she murmured. This was not the time to antagonize Jason by hurling accusations at him. They were neither one in a frame of mind to be cool and rational.

"It's all right," he muttered. "I guess we're both testy."

She nodded. When she looked up at him, she saw he was gazing down at her intently. Even in the hazy light that filtered in from the living room, Janet could see the expression on his face slowly change. Then he bent to kiss her. She responded gradually, meeting his first light kisses before joining him in a deeper, more passionate one. His hands played in her hair as his mouth wandered on hers. For the moment he demanded nothing more.

Then Jason scooped her off her feet and laid her back on the bed; he followed her down. When he shifted his weight against her, it was in a way that made Janet feel a surge of anticipation as the lean length of his masculine form fitted to the soft, female curves of her own body. Instinctively, she arched against him. He stroked the tender skin at the nape of her neck with a skillful finger while his lips continued to possess hers.

"I want you, Janet," he said, his lips moving against her as he spoke. It was a statement that brooked no argument had she been of a mind to—but she was not.

As if sensing her unspoken agreement, he turned his attention to pulling her clothes from her. The black and tan T-shirt was discarded on the floor without another glance. His eyes never left her body as his expert fingers slid to her back and unhooked the catch of her bra.

It fell from her and was tossed unnoticed onto the floor. She watched his eyes move from her mouth to the rosy peaks of her breasts and he bent to caress one saluting nipple, taking it between his teeth and moving it slowly back and forth with deliberate provocativeness.

Janet savored the sensation, a blend of blissful pain that made her whole body ache for more. His hands stroked her bare flat stomach, moving steadily lower as her eyes drifted shut and she gave herself over to the exquisite feel of his touch. She felt as if she were under the influence of a strong narcotic, potent enough to make her forget everything except the throbbing feelings his skillful hands were awakening.

As his strong hands caressed her, Janet could hear Jason's heightened breathing. She thrilled to the sound of it and to the touch of his fingers trailing across her body. They were warm with longing while he searched her with a sure, exciting touch.

Her own movements—the hand she brought up to touch his face as his lips lingered on her breast and the slight arch of her body against his—were like the motions of a ballet performed in slow motion. It was one of those moments when a natural sense of what was correct guided her; she was sure of her part as he led her into secret realms and he aroused her to a pitch of emotion. She wanted it to continue endlessly.

"Jason," she murmured his name mindlessly. "Jason, Jason."

His lips returned to hers and caught them in a tantalizing embrace. The pulsating trembling coursing through her intensified and she thrilled to the touch of him, and the feel of his hands on her yielding body. His fingers deftly moved the zipper of her slacks downward and then slid them off her.

Raising his head, he straightened and turned his attention to removing the rest of her clothes. She looked up at him through passion-laden eyes and smiled.

Jason bent back to her mouth and placed a hard kiss on it, quick and masterful. "I'll be gentle," he promised.

She nodded dumbly and immersed herself once again into the delight of his touch. A moment later she was naked on the bed and he stood over her, pulling off his own clothes. In the darkness he looked like a colossus, she thought, as she studied him through half-open lashes. At the sight of him standing over her looking so tall she knew an instant of fright. It was erased when he lay down beside her again and whispered, "You're tense. Don't worry, I won't hurt you."

Janet nodded again. She believed him and she was even more sure of his words as his hands moved gently and then more insistently while she lost herself to the feeling he evoked. Jason's lips came down on hers while he shifted her on the bed. Her eyes drifted closed again and she waited for him to bring them together.

A sharp, shrill noise intruded into their sensual world of unreality. Janet stiffened at the sound and Jason muttered a curse.

"Damn phone," he grumbled as he stood and hastily pulled his clothes on.

A moment later Janet heard him speaking to someone on the telephone. "Yes. They found her where?" he demanded in disbelief. "I'm coming."

Janet rose quickly and donned her own clothes. She rushed into the living room just as Jason put the receiver down. "What is it?" she asked. "Is Susan all right?"

"She's fine," he replied. "They found her in the back of one of the farm hand's truck. Apparently she climbed in it and rode into town when one of them left last night. She must have fallen asleep during the drive. Anyway, she was still there this morning. She's at the ranch house now."

"Oh," Janet replied. "I guess you had better go to her."

"Yes," he agreed shortly. A moment later he was gone, with no further word to her.

Janet watched his car pull out before she turned back toward the bedroom. It seemed her encounters with Jason were destined to be fraught with interruptions, she considered moodily. It was a thought which might have seemed humorous under other circumstances, but it did not strike her as such at the present. It was even less amusing when she considered she had nearly slept with a man whom she had refused to date not twenty-four hours earlier.

Although Bessie was fun to visit with and Janet made daily walks along the river as a diversion, there was no denying the fact she was hungry for the company of someone nearer her age.

When Ron arrived Saturday, Janet met him at the door with a wide smile. "Come on in," she invited. "I packed a lunch, but the lead in the sandwiches has made the basket so heavy I can hardly pick it up. Why don't you give it a try?"

"Your sandwiches sound wonderful. In case we run out of them I brought some pieces of fried chicken." He walked into the kitchen and stooped to pick up the picnic basket she had packed. "Wow!" he said as his eyes widened. "What's in here?"

"Little heavy, isn't it? Just a bottle of wine, a few glasses, kitchen plates since I didn't have any paper ones, silverware—the usual."

"I see," he murmured. "Well, let's go."

Janet followed him out to the car carrying blankets and towels. After Ron put the basket in the trunk and slid in on the driver's side, they started off down the road.

"Where are we going?" she asked.

"Great Salt Plains Lake. You brought your bathing suit, didn't you?"

She nodded.

"Good. There are some nice places to picnic around the lake and after that we may try our hand at digging some selenite crystals that grow in the sandy salt crust by the lake. How does that sound?"

"Terrific," she sighed, leaning back in contentment. She was glad to be out of her house; she would have dug graves if it would have afforded her some company.

had resolved she would have nothing further to do with him even if he did call her.

When she stepped back into the house after a lazy walk along the river and heard the phone ringing, she was tempted not to answer it. However, she decided, if it was Jason, she might as well have the satisfaction of telling him what her feelings toward him were. Letting the driftwood she was carrying slide out of her arms on the front step, she stepped inside and picked up the receiver.

"Hello," she said tersely.

"Hi, remember me?"

Janet made a wry smile to herself. Remember him? She knew only one man who would call her in such a friendly voice and that was Ron. His cheerful words bore no resemblance to Jason's deep, resonant voice.

"I remember you, Ron," she laughed.

"Good. I'm calling because I just got into the motel here in Alva. I was gone a lot longer than I had hoped I would be. I'll be busy tomorrow, but I thought you might like to go on a picnic Saturday."

"That would be nice."

"Good. I'll pick you up at nine on Saturday morning and we'll make a day of it."

"Sounds perfect," she replied.

He chuckled at her enthusiasm. "I'll see you then."

"Bye," she said. As she put the receiver down she considered that a date with Ron was a lucky event. She had begun to think she would not be hearing from him again. After all, he might not ever have been sent back out to western Oklahoma. She was glad he had. She needed companionship right now.

CHAPTER 6

Secure in the knowledge that Jason would call, Janet immersed herself in jobs around the house. She cleaned the little cottage from top to bottom that day. The following day she painted the bathroom a crisp ivory with delicate mauve trim. When she had not heard from Jason by the next afternoon, Janet abandoned the house and drove to Alva to shop for new towels and curtains for the bathroom. On the morning after that, she potted geraniums and placed them carefully in the window boxes around the house. By that afternoon her feelings toward Jason had altered from a patient waiting to hear from him to a smoldering sense of ill use. Damn the man! He could at least have the decency to let her know how Susan was and give her the full details of what happened to precipitate her flight.

Actually, Janet had learned all the finer points of the story from Bessie and the check-out girl at the grocery store, but that did not lessen her bruised feelings toward Jason. Considering what had nearly happened between them, she had expected to be seeing him again on a social level.

By the second week after Susan's disappearance, Janet's resentment against Jason had galvanized; she

She shook her head to clear it of such thoughts. Why was she even thinking about Jason at a time like this? She should be thankful that Susan had been found and that she was all right. She was anxious for Jason to call and give her further news of Susan.

As he drove, Ron told her of the work that had tied him up in the office and she relayed the local events of interest that had occurred in his absence.

"Have you been bored?" he asked when she paused.

"Yes and no. At times I wake up and think 'I have the whole day to myself' and the idea sounds great. I've had time to read some new authors I've been wanting to study and I've fixed up the house to make it more comfortable. Still," she finished, "I guess every once in awhile I just need someone to talk to."

"Well, now that I'm back you can always call me when that mood strikes you."

"Thanks, I will."

"Here we are," he said as they drove into a picnic area.

Janet turned her gaze out across the pure blue water. "It's beautiful," she said, her eyes searching the expanse of shimmering water and blinking at the reflection from behind it. "What's that white flat area behind the lake? It almost seems to have wavy heat lines rising from it."

"That's the salt flats where we'll dig crystals. Up close it looks like it's covered with sleet. Those waves you're talking about the early explorers called 'looming.' That's a nautical term for a mirage, I think."

"Oh," she said, giving another squinted look at the dazzling white sands before letting her eyes skim back across the blue water again. She turned back to Ron. "It's funny, but when I first came to western Oklahoma I thought there was nothing of interest within a hundred miles of the town. Since then I've discovered there are gypsum caverns not ten miles from Freedom that house an alabaster so rare there is an example of it in the Smithsonian. And thirty miles away is Little Sahara Recreation area which has some of the most majestic-looking sand dunes I've ever seen, and totally unspoiled. It seems you can have the best of both worlds here."

Ron laughed. "There may be a thing or two of interest, but when you're ninety, I don't think you'll still find that the area abounds with wonders. That's why you should be thinking about moving to a city. Which brings me to my question. What have you heard from the Tulsa area schools?"

"Nothing yet, but I expect I will any day. Hey, why don't we break out the fried chicken and potato chips and start eating? I'm starving."

"At your service." He mock saluted and opened the trunk to lift out the basket and carry it to the picnic table.

They ate their lunch in leisurely fashion, bantering with each other as they ate. When they finished their meal, they packed up the remains and stowed it in the tiny trunk of the car. They waited an hour for the food to settle, sitting comfortably on the hood of Ron's small car and talking easily before they changed into their bathing suits in the nearby rest rooms. When she emerged, dressed in a one-piece coral suit, Ron was waiting for her. They walked to the shoreline and eased themselves into the cool water at the edge of the lake.

The heavy concentration of natural salt in the lake had a buoying effect and Janet swam and floated about the water until her eyes smarted from the tingling salt before she retreated back to the sandy beach.

"Why don't we go around to the other side of the

lake and see about digging some crystals?" Ron suggested as he sat down on the sand beside her.

"Okay." She ran a hand through the half-dry hair that fell casually about her face from its natural center part before standing and starting back to the picnic area.

After changing back into her clothes she wedged herself in the bucket seat beside Ron. She glanced around at the few vacationers at scattered picnic tables and then turned curiously back to Ron. Why hadn't he started the car?

As she turned Janet realized the answer to that question. Ron's face was close to hers, poised for a kiss. Surprised, Janet made no protest as he brought his lips to meet hers. His mouth moved across hers, tentatively, before he wrapped his arms around her neck and drew her closer into his embrace. It was a smooth, careful kiss, as if he was afraid to do anything that might offend her. She reassured him by putting her arms around his neck and drawing him closer to her.

"I wasn't sure you'd want to see me after I'd been gone so long," he said, pulling back to look intently in her face. "I thought you might have found some other guy you were dating exclusively."

She shook her head. "No, I'm available."

"I'm glad" he said as he brought his mouth back to hers. His kiss was not demanding or forceful, but it was thorough, and when Janet emerged, she felt a glow of contentment. "I guess we had better go dig some crystals before I get sidetracked," he said regretfully.

"Yes, we'd better," she teased. She settled back on

her side of the car as Ron drove out of the picnic area and started across the spillway of the dam. Then he followed the country lanes that were well marked with signs leading to the gem-collecting area.

"Are you sure you know what you're doing?" Janet laughed an hour later as she stood knee deep in a hole filled with muddy water and splashed the water against the sides of the pit. "This is the most unusual date I've ever had."

"Just keep throwing water on it," Ron said from beside her. "Don't try to break the crystals off yet. The more we can get worked loose from the sand, the bigger and nicer the cluster we can get."

"You're the boss," she replied cheerfully. "This takes me back to my mud pie days."

"You don't mind, do you?" Ron asked, straightening suddenly and regarding her seriously. "I didn't think to ask you. I guess it is pretty dirty work."

"Don't be ridiculous. I'm having a good time," she reassured him.

"You're a good sport," he praised.

She nodded agreeably and continued washing the protruding crystals with the muddy water. Actually, she was enjoying herself more than she had in some time. Ron was a comfortable person to be with. They chatted when they felt like it and in between worked silently on their tasks.

It was the same easy feeling she had always felt with Lars, as if whatever she wanted to give was enough and he wouldn't push for more. That was good for the present, she considered. After her last encounter with Jason she was too confused by men to want one pushing her. It had become obvious to her over the last few days that the ringing of the telephone had saved her from making a serious mistake with Jason. If he didn't think enough of her even to call back, it could only mean that he had intended her to be a one-night stand. She scooped her hands into the brown water and flung a particularly brisk scoop of water at the crystals.

"Whoa! Those things are delicate. Don't throw water too hard," Ron cautioned.

"I'm sorry. I guess I was thinking about something else."

"Care to talk about it?" he asked without looking up from his work.

She shook her head. "No, it's nothing really."

"I won't pry, but it does seem that something has been bothering you today."

"Pretty observant, aren't you?" Janet asked. Men seemed to be headed in that direction lately, she rued. Jason could also read her thoughts. She needed to develop a more creditable veneer.

"I think we've gotten enough of the crystal loose to remove it," Ron said.

Janet looked at him with a quick smile. She knew he was deliberately changing the subject because he had guessed she didn't want to discuss the cause of her distraction.

He leaned over from the cluster he had been working on to help her gently pull a foot-long mass of small selenite blades from the water. They were covered with mud and dripping brown water. "They'll look a lot better when you get them washed up," he informed her. "I'll show you how. You have to be careful with them because they're very fragile."

"I will," she told him. "Now what about yours? I'll help you."

After they removed Ron's cluster of crystals they drove back to the camping area and washed some of the sand and grime off themselves in the rest rooms.

It wasn't until nearly three in the afternoon that they started back toward Freedom, sunburned and windswept, but talking cheerfully about their day.

"Do you mind if I stop to see one of the landowners?" Ron asked as they drove eastward. "We're going to be drilling on his property this week and I always like to let the owners know before we come in even though we have rights-of-entry."

"Who is the man you want to see?" Janet suspected the question sounded odd, but she wanted to make sure it was not Jason before she committed herself to stopping.

"His name is Drew Worth. Do you mind if we stop?" he repeated.

"No, of course not." She didn't, as long as it wasn't Jason Stewart.

"Thanks. Sorry to have to spend time on business concerns, but when we get back to your house we can have time to ourselves." He swung the car off the highway and drove over a cattle guard, the metal rungs rattling as the tires rolled across them. Black angus cattle looked up from their grazing to stare curiously at the car as they drove through a green pasture.

"Good thing I'm not in my pickup," Ron laughed. "In the winter the ranchers bring feed out in their pickups for the cattle. So now the stock all follow a truck when they see one. I don't know why they hope for a bale of hay when they have thousands of acres of pastureland to feed on, but they do."

He steered the car across another cattle guard and stopped at a low, buff brick ranch house set back among a few tall trees that were present as a windbreak on the sweeping prairie landscape.

"I'll just be a second," he promised.

"Okay." Janet sat idly in the car until Ron rejoined her a few minutes later.

"Well, I found out what I wanted to know, but it's going to entail another stop. You don't mind, do you?"

"Where?"

"Jason Stewart's. This man's tin whistle bridge washed out in the rain so he has no way for us to get across the river. We'll have to go in through Jason's property."

"Ron—" Janet began. She stopped. How could she ask him to drive back later when they were practically there now?

"I know what you're going to say," he assured her. "You don't want to spend all your time sitting in a car. Don't worry. Since you know Jason you can go in his house."

"But I don't want to go into *his* house," she objected.

Ron made no reply, but the puzzled glance he flicked at her made Janet realize how terribly rude her statement had sounded. "I'm sorry," she told him contritely. "I didn't mean that to sound the way it did. I don't mind if you stop at Jason's house, but I'd rather wait in the car."

"Suit yourself," Ron shrugged. He gave her another curious look as he turned off the highway and started down the long drive to Jason's house. A few minutes later they were parked in the driveway beside the silver Mercedes. "Are you sure you don't want to come in?" Ron asked, leaning down to look in her window.

"No, I'll wait."

"I'll be back in a minute."

Janet watched him walk up to the house and saw the door open a moment later. Then the dark, round housekeeper gestured Ron into the house. Janet leaned back against the headrest and closed her eyes. She really didn't care how long Ron was gone as long as she didn't have to see Jason.

As if on cue, she heard a lazy voice drawl softly, "Well, if it isn't Sleeping Beauty."

Janet's eyelids sprang open. Jason was bending over her window, looking in. His face was unnervingly close to hers and she drew back slightly. "Ron is in the house waiting for you," she said crisply.

"Why didn't you want to come in?" he asked.

"Why should I?" she replied indifferently. She thought it should be perfectly clear to him why she didn't want to be in his house. She felt a little foolish even to be sitting in his driveway. If he was so anxious to have her inside, why was he waiting till he found her on his doorstep to make the invitation? she wondered waspishly.

"Don't you want to see Susan and assure yourself she is all right?" He seemed perplexed by her attitude.

"I have already heard by way of rumor that she is."

"A poor way to obtain information," he observed.

"I like it," she responded. "I think you and I should communicate entirely by rumor, if at all."

"Do I sense an edge of hostility in that sweet voice of yours?" he asked with an assessing look at her through narrowed eyes.

"You might. It's hard to tell what you can find in people. I imagine you are able to attribute to them just exactly what you wish to see. If, by some freak of nature, they don't make the responses you had expected, I think you goad them into that reaction." She looked at him defiantly.

"What the hell does that mean?" he demanded impatiently.

"It means I have the distinct impression you hope I'm angry with you. Isn't that what you set out to make me? I assumed that was why you never called to tell me how Susan was after I had spent an exhausting night looking for her with you."

"That was not the only thing you did that night—or were prepared to do," he reminded her bluntly. "But we were interrupted. Now, I'd like to know why you are suddenly mad at me when we parted in good humor?"

"I am susceptible to change, whatever my feelings might have been at the time. Considering it has been three weeks since I saw or heard from you I have had plenty of time to make that change."

"There is a logical explanation of why I didn't call you. Would you like to hear it?"

"No, I'm not interested," she said flatly.

"There you are," Ron called, coming toward the car in easy strides.

"I was just inviting Miss Matthews to come inside," Jason said with a smile. He opened the door of the car as he spoke.

"Yes, Janet," Ron added. "Come in. It's silly for you to sit in the car."

Janet acquiesced with stiff politeness.

CHAPTER 7

Janet absently dusted the pictures atop the television, listening to the soft country music on the radio and humming to herself. She was in a much more cheerful frame of mind today than she had been two weeks ago when she had been forced to join Ron in Jason's living room and feel Jason's eyes upon her as she sat stiffly and silently in the sculpted brown chair.

Two lunches were carefully packed in twin brown paper bags, setting on a chair by the door. Janet was dusting just to pass time until eleven o'clock. Then she would go out to where Ron was working and they would have an impromptu picnic.

She wasn't sure exactly where Ron was, but he had given her detailed instructions how to find the rig when he had called her last night to suggest that she come. The other workers, he had told her, would go into town for their lunches so she would be alone with him.

Janet glanced at her watch. Five minutes until eleven. She put the dusting rag down in her cleaning pail and carried it into the kitchen to deposit it under the kitchen sink. Rising, she brushed her hands against her pale orange cotton shorts that revealed her tanned legs. She carefully inspected the white knit top that tied below her bustline for any signs of dirt. Satisfied that all was in order, she gave her bronze locks a final pat and started out the door.

Janet headed the little red car out the road Ron had directed. As she drove she referred from time to time to a piece of notebook paper with scribbled directions. She turned off the main road as Ron had instructed at a gate that bore a hand-painted sign proclaiming, "Here lies the body of Lester Bates; he forgot to shut my gates."

Janet smiled to herself as she slid from the car and opened the five-bar gate, swinging it back easily. Hopping back into the car, she drove through and reclosed the gate and continued on down the bumpy dirt road. She concentrated on taking the right branches as the trail faded into a dim path. Finally only an almost indistinguishable section of faintly beaten down grass remained as an indication that anyone had ever traveled the route before her. Pulling up at the rig she jumped out of the car.

"I'm here," she called.

Silence.

"I'm here, Ron," she repeated, louder, and heard the faintest echo of her words come back to her eerily from down the draw. Janet looked around uncomfortably. Was Ron hiding and preparing to jump out and surprise her?

She walked slowly to the back of the large truck and looked curiously at the round hole, about the size of a plate, being spiraled into the ground. Walking around to the front of the large truck, she noticed a piece of white paper attached to the windshield wiper, flapping in the gentle breeze.

Janet climbed up the side of the truck and plucked the note from the wiper.

    Janet—

    It read:

    had to go into town. I shouldn't be gone long. Wait for me.   Ron.

She folded the note and climbed back down to the ground. Seating herself in the car with her legs swung out to the side, she turned on the engine and flipped on the radio, adjusting the volume up.

"What are you doing here?"

Janet jumped at the sound of a man's gruff voice and swiveled her head upward. Jason was looming over her, a magnificent bay horse beside him.

"Oh, it's you," she said, relief mixed with chagrin in her voice.

"What are you doing here?" he demanded again. She could hear the irritation in his voice.

"It's not any of your business," she fired back at him.

"I think since you are on my land it is my business," he replied evenly. He did not wait for her to reply as he turned his attention to the restless horse. He led it over to the rig and tied it beneath a shady tree before returning to her.

"Now," he pursued, leaning on the side of her little car, "why are you here?"

"I am meeting Ron for lunch. He had to go into town so I'm waiting for him."

"Ron," he said the word as if he were considering it carefully. "Just what is he to you?"

As Jason spoke, he took in her scanty outfit, one that had been chosen for its coolness on a hot, sunny day. His eyes assessed her from her sandaled feet up to her cuffed shorts and further up to linger on the midriff revealed by her brief top. His gaze was almost insulting in its casual surveyal.

She made no answer to his question—none was called for, she thought. It was not Jason Stewart's concern what Ron was to her. If Jason wanted to throw her off his property, that was his affair, but she had no intention of replying to any personal questions.

"You haven't answered me." His arctic blue eyes were riveted to her face.

"I don't think I remember what the question was," she said with deliberate languidness.

"Don't you?" Jason's eyes narrowed. "Don't play with me, Janet."

"I'm not," she snapped. "I happen to believe that it is none of your business what sort of relationship I may have going with Ron. Although," she added, "it's a more satisfying arrangement than you and I could ever hoped to have had."

Jason's face registered an odd expression of surprise.

Janet thought there had been a flash of something else before it was once again drawn into a hard mask, all emotion concealed. What had that look been? She groped in her mind for the word to describe his naked reaction to her words. Had she seen hurt in Jason's face? Or was she mistaken, reading meanings where there were none?

But if he had really betrayed such an emotion, he gave no evidence of it as he told her with biting scorn,

"If you want to have your little fun with some city boy, then you can do it in his motel room, but not on my ranch. Now get out of here."

Janet gave a cool nod. "Whatever you say," she replied haughtily. She swung her legs back into the car and started the engine, waiting until he stepped away from the car before putting it in reverse and backing around in the long grass. Then she followed the trail back to the main road.

As she drove, Janet considered how ironic it was that she met Jason by accident when she no longer wanted to see him. There had been a time—immediately after Susan's disappearance—when she had been desperate to see him. It was not something that she liked to admit, especially now, but she knew it was true. She had wanted to be with him again and, yes, she had wanted them to finish what had been started in her bedroom.

Her relationship with Ron was a good friendship, but she knew she could never permit it to go any deeper than that until she had rid herself completely of her feelings for Jason. Those emotions should have evaporated on their own, starved for lack of attention, but they had not.

Why had nothing further developed between herself and Jason? He had said there was a reason he had not called her after the night they had spent looking for Susan, but Janet had not been in a mood to find out if there really was or if he only meant to give her a plausible excuse. At any rate, for all she knew he was still dating Georgia. Janet didn't think her ego could stand playing second fiddle to *her*. Why did Jason play these games? she asked herself as she stopped to open the gate. She drove through it and shut it behind her, still considering the pain Jason had caused her.

Her mind slowed at the word "pain" and a cog slipped into place. That look on Jason's face, could it have been hurt? Perhaps he was jealous of Ron. Was that why he didn't want her to see him? Jason had never said he didn't want her to see Ron, she reminded herself, he had merely stated he didn't want her on his land. It was doubtful Jason was or ever had been jealous of anyone.

Janet was on her way back to town before she remembered Ron's message asking her to wait for him. If she didn't pass him on the road, she could surely find him in such a tiny town, she decided. She certainly wasn't going back out to the rig. She drove on to Freedom and located Ron in the hardware store.

"Hi," he greeted her in surprise as he looked up from paying for a purchase. "Did you get tired of waiting for me?"

"No," she smiled. "I thought you might be tied up here longer than you had thought so I came on in." There was no reason to relate her altercation with Jason.

"It's probably a good thing you did," he confided candidly. "I hate to say this, but I don't think I can make lunch today anyway. I'm going to have to drive to Alva to get something else I need. I don't know how long I'll be gone."

She nodded. "Sure, maybe some other time."

"Yeah. I'll call you," he said as she turned to leave. "Thanks, you really are a good sport. You take everything in such good humor."

Not everything, Janet considered as she returned

to her house. With Ron, it was true, she was usually in a better frame of mind than she was with a certain other man. She realized that she was able to maintain an easygoing relationship with Ron because his demands were so few. They kissed, sure, but he seemed to know that she was not ready to accept anything more than that so he never tried.

Janet changed into an old white shirt and jeans and returned to the task she had been involved in the past few days. She was working out in the back yard carefully stripping paint off an old oak dresser she had found in a used furniture store. She had just come back into the house and was cleaning up when she heard a knock on the door. Janet wiped her hands with a towel and went to answer it. Bessie was standing on the doorstep with a foil-covered dish in her hands.

"Come in," Janet said, opening the door as she spoke.

"I brought you a pie," Bessie greeted her. "It's rhubarb, I hope you like it. Lots of folks don't, but I've always been partial to it."

"I've never tasted rhubarb, but I'm sure I'll like it."

"It's like a cross between sweet and sour," Bessie explained, surrendering the dessert to Janet. "It may make your mouth pucker a little, but the flavor is good. It's something like gooseberries."

"I've never eaten them either," Janet confessed, carrying the still-warm pie into the kitchen.

"What do they eat back where you come from?" Bessie asked curiously.

Janet laughed as she returned from the kitchen.

"We managed all right. Sit down, Bessie. Let me get you a cool drink and I'll cut us both a piece of pie."

Bessie gave silent assent by sinking onto the sofa and looking around the living room with interest. "The plants make it look real nice and homey, hon," she complimented. "I don't have much luck with indoor plants, but I can sure raise them outdoors. Back in the dust-bowl days I got so I could raise a lot of things that other folks couldn't get to grow."

"That must have been something to see, the land drying up and blowing away and all the people piling furniture and belongings into trucks and heading to California."

"Yeah," the old woman said with a reminiscent look in her faded blue eyes. "It was a lot different than today." She shook her head and brought herself out of her reverie. "But times are better now. I notice," she continued with a sly look as Janet returned from the kitchen, handing the old woman a plate with a piece of pie, "that times are good for you, too. I see that brown car parked here almost every day. Is it some fellow visiting?"

Janet smiled and nodded. "Yes, that's Ron, the man who works for the government. He stops by to watch television or talk sometimes on his way to the motel in Alva."

"That's nice," Bessie said shortly.

"He really is a pleasant person even if he does work for the government," Janet defended.

"I'm sure he is," Bessie said noncommittally. "I used to," she pursued, "see Jason Stewart's car parked here every once in a while."

"He was here a time or two," Janet replied vaguely. That was the trouble with a small town; everyone knew everyone's business and they made no bones about asking questions about anything that intrigued them. And Jason obviously interested Bessie. "Have you heard from Rita?" Janet asked to change the subject.

"She's fine, back in Tulsa and dating some man who drives a taxi. I don't know what's going to become of her," Bessie lamented as if she were speaking of a teen-age girl instead of a middle-aged woman. "She just can't seem to settle on one man and stay with him. Kind of like you," Bessie smoothly brought the conversation back to Janet.

Janet finished the last bite of her pie and stood, picking up her plate and carrying it to the kitchen as she spoke. "I'm going to Alva some afternoon this week. Would you like to go with me?"

"Changing the subject again," the old woman noted mildly. "All right. I can take a hint. I'd like to go to Alva. I've been thinking about getting some curtains to go with my new carpet and I could look there at the dime store."

"Good. I'll be glad for the company."

Bessie rose as Janet returned to the living room. "Well, I've got to go now, hon. Thanks for the drink."

The elderly lady shuffled out the door as Janet held it open, watching her make the short walk to her own house three doors down. For a woman of her age, and Janet guessed Bessie must be in her late seventies, she still had a lot of life left in her. In her lifetime, she had probably seen a great many things.

Of course, Janet pursued her train of thought as she closed the door, in her own twenty-six years she had also seen many things. Even Susan had witnessed a great deal more of life—far more than most little girls her age. And Jason, what had he known? Janet knew his mother had left him when he was young, although she had taken her other child. He had probably always felt the bitterness of that rejection.

Janet's thoughts were interrupted by the insistent ringing of the telephone. She walked to the phone and picked it up. "Hello," she said.

"Is this Miss Matthews?" a woman asked.

"Yes, it is," she replied. It sounded as if it were a long distance phone call.

"This is Mrs. Lindsey. I'm with the Tulsa school district. We received a letter from you several weeks ago and I'm sorry we have been so long in processing your application. Are you still interested?"

Janet thought quickly. Was she still looking for employment outside Freedom? She had not given the matter a great deal of thought lately. But there was nothing to hold her here. "Yes, Mrs. Lindsey," she replied, "I'm still interested." After she said the words, Janet felt a definite sinking of her spirits. Everyone was afraid of new jobs, she reassured herself.

"Ordinarily," Mrs. Lindsey continued in a crisp, professional voice, "it would be necessary for you to come in for an interview. However, I am a personal friend of both the school principal and the superintendent at Freedom. I've spoken with both of them and you come very highly recommended. Of course, this does not mean you have been selected; there are two other well-qualified candidates, but you'll be hearing from us."

"I see," Janet said.

"Good-bye."

"Good-bye," Janet repeated before a click sounded on the other end of the line.

A job in Tulsa. Leave Freedom. She stood and paced the room in agitation. Why should she be so restless and uncertain? Tulsa schools undoubtedly paid more than she made now. Added to that, there would be any number of things to do in a city, whereas there was nothing to do in this little town. Finally, she told herself, she would have a chance to meet more people her age. Still she was uncertain.

When Ron stopped by after work that evening, she told him the news.

"You don't seem very thrilled by the prospect of going to Tulsa," he noted.

"Well," she said slowly, "they haven't actually offered me a job, but I'm not sure I would accept if they did."

After seating himself on the red and blue sofa, Ron patted the seat beside him. "Sit down, Janet. Let's talk about this."

She obeyed, taking a place beside him and waiting for him to speak.

"Why did you apply for the job in the first place?" he began.

Janet recalled the threat Jason had made to have her fired which had prompted thoughts of seeking a job elsewhere. Of course, he had later retracted his words so she was assured of a position if she wished to stay. Did she want to remain? she asked herself.

"You're not sure why you applied," Ron said. It was a statement, not a question.

"I know it sounds crazy. I should have a definite goal in mind and be working toward it. I always have before. But now, somehow, I feel as if a part of me belongs here even though the opportunity for more money and advancement may not be present. I think Freedom offers compensations that I might not find elsewhere."

"Like what?" he asked softly.

Janet held his steady gaze as she replied, she wanted to be honest with him as well as with herself. "It's safe here and I'm not afraid to live alone," she began slowly. "I can come and go at night and that's a freedom I would lose in a city. Then, of course, I've grown attached to the people out here. Since I don't have a real home anywhere else, I've come to think of this as my home. This house is for sale so I could buy it at a reasonable price and continue to live here if I wanted to," she pursued.

"Is there something else, Janet?" he asked quietly.

"I'm not sure," she replied, still meeting his eyes. Ron was a perceptive person; he understood a great deal about her and she sensed he knew there was something standing between himself and her. He had never asked before, but she knew he would now.

"I've never pushed you, but I need to know. I won't be coming to western Oklahoma very much after this summer is over. I'd like for you to move to Tulsa, but only if that's what you want. Don't do it just to make me happy."

"I'll have to give it some more thought, Ron. And, of course," she added with a light laugh, "I'll have to see if they offer me a job. I'd feel rather silly calling to accept a job they have no intention of giving me."

He chuckled. "I understand. Now," he continued, rising as he spoke, "let's go out and get something to eat. I'm starving." He rose as she did. "Just remember," he added as she picked up her purse, "Tulsa would be a great place to start your future."

As she lay in her bed that night, tossing uneasily from one side to the other, Janet wasn't at all certain Tulsa was where she wanted to spend her future. It seemed as if the West had claimed her. The red earth that rolled across the plains before making a dramatic drop—awesome and colorful in shades of maroon, red, and orange—down to the river, seemed somehow to be a part of her. And the little town of Freedom, as inconspicuous as a speck of dust on the rolling plains, had become her refuge.

Janet sat up in bed and thumped the pillow into a more comfortable shape. She lay back restlessly. The night was going to be long, she could tell, and through the slow hours she considered why she didn't want to leave Freedom.

The real reason, she knew, had nothing to do with the picturesque little frontier town or the rugged beauty of the desert coming into bloom. The true reason was not the scenery at all. It was, quite simply, a man.

The man, as rugged and individualistic as the ground he moved across, was Jason Stewart. Janet had not seen him since he had ordered her off his land three weeks ago, but the memory of him was still very much present. Each time she thought of him a nameless longing surged through her and she felt the aching desire to be held in his arms. She loved him.

Janet turned over on the bed again, savagely smoothing the rumpled covers. Jason Stewart felt nothing for her. And the sooner she was able to push him from her mind the better her life was going to be. It was pointless and childish to hold onto the hope he could ever care for her. It was a hope so faint as to be lost.

But in the disquieting sleep that finally settled over her, the hope blossomed again into a real yearning as she saw a dream-induced Jason striding toward her, smiling at her and opening his arms to catch her up in them.

When she awoke very early the next morning, a faint smile was playing on her lips as she lay curled on the bed, her eyes tracing a pattern on the tiled ceiling. She brought herself back to reality by degrees. The smile faded slowly as Janet realized it had all been a dream. Jason Stewart would never come to her with open arms. And if he did, it would be for a night's amusement only.

Disturbed, she pulled herself from the bed and padded to the bathroom in bare feet. As she brushed her teeth she considered the events of yesterday. Ron had told her what she didn't want to hear, but it was true for all that. There was nothing for her in Freedom.

Her thoughts circled in her mind, but she could come to no conclusion. She needed to get out—go for a brisk walk and clear her mind. It was just past five in the morning so she could have the world to herself.

She pulled on a kelly green knit shirt and beige slacks. Flinging a light jacket over her shoulder she started out into the morning mist and walked through the sleeping town toward the river. She crossed the long bridge, watching in fascination as the sun rose in the east with a faint emergence of purple that turned to a rich hue of pink and finally burst across the sky in a blaze of orange and gold. As she reached the end of the bridge she stopped to stare awestruck at the wonder of the sight still unfolding before her.

Nature, dramatic and powerful, had her in its grip. And she liked the feeling. She turned and ran off the bridge, down the gentle slope to the river. There her steps were slowed by the heavy dry sand; she stopped in the thick sand and looked around, smiling to herself.

How many other people, she wondered, had seen a sunrise like the one she had just witnessed? Nothing could go wrong in the world today—not in a world with such a splendid sunrise. Her troubles were tightly corralled at the back of her mind. Tomorrow she would be back in the realm of world affairs, but today she had a rendezvous with nature, undisturbed by man or thoughts of him.

She walked across the sandy bed, splashing through the trickle of stream and feeling the muddy ground around it give beneath her feet. It was an exciting feeling, but not alarming; there was not enough water present to make real quicksand. She reached the base of the mighty cliff that towered upward, bounding the south side of the river. Above her flashes of the shiny gypsum rock glinted at her, beckoning to her.

Tying her jacket around her waist by the sleeves, Janet began a slow ascent of the cliff. The rocks, invited her upward with their natural stepping spots, and she placed each foot carefully, holding onto the boulders around her as she made her way forward. By the time she had scaled a third of the way up the escarpment, she was gasping for breath. She stopped to rest, looking back down and feeling for the first time a shiver of worry. Was it safe to be climbing these rocks? Some of the smaller pebbles and cobbles had dislodged under her feet and she had heard them go hurtling to the ground behind her, making soft thuds in the sand as they landed. Could the large rocks move also?

The sight of a curious little pointed object at her foot drew her attention away from the thought of danger. Clinging to her hold with one hand she bent to pick up the stone. It was an arrowhead, made by some Indian hundreds, perhaps thousands, of years ago. She turned it over in her hand in wonder and then looked farther up the cliff. Perhaps there were more artifacts higher up. This one must have washed down from the top of the bluff. There might even be hide scrapers or pottery up above.

Spurred on by her discovery and the hope of finding more, Janet turned her attention back to the climb, carefully putting the arrowhead in the pocket of her shirt before starting her steady progress upward.

She was almost two thirds of the way up when she stopped and looked back again. She was panting hard from her exertion. From where she was she could see the whole of the town of Freedom, laid out like a neat little toy town; a truck that drove down Main Street was no bigger than an inch. She drew her eyes away from the sight; there would be time to appreciate all this from the summit. Putting a hand on a large rock she began to pull herself upward.

And then everything happened at once. The rock above her slipped and began sliding toward her, slowly and then faster. Janet screamed as she flattened her body against another rock. The boulder fell past her, missing her by inches and grazing her knee. She looked at it in terror, watching it fall the height of a ten-story building before hitting the river below.

And then she heard rumbling noises above her. With her heart in her mouth, Janet turned terror-stricken eyes upward. Not twenty feet above her head, a whole section of the wall was pulling out away from the cliff. A scattering of cobbles and small boulders was tumbling downward, forerunners of the massive chunks of rock preparing to fall.

The roar of the impending avalanche, the popping sounds as the small rocks fell upon one another in the river bed below, and Janet's own screams, were the last things she was fully aware of.

Everything blurred for her then and she was only vaguely conscious of the huge rocks cascading past her and of the dizzying pain she felt as rocks bounced off the hands she had raised protectively to cover her head. She felt the rain of silt and dirt that accompanied the slide.

It was over in a matter of minutes. A section of wall thirty-feet wide and twenty-feet high was gone, had vanished from above her. Instead, it lay crumbled on the valley floor below. The river still lapped placidly by, disturbed only because it had to make its way around massive boulders.

Janet put a hand to her heart and willed herself to slow the beating in her chest before she exploded from its alarming pace. She noted dispassionately that her arms were bruised and bleeding. She could feel a knot rising on her head and, worst of all, a throbbing pain was pulsating in her leg. She transferred her hypnotic stare from the sight in the river channel to her leg and stared at it like a bystander witnessing a calamity that has befallen someone else.

There, arched across her ankle, was a boulder fully the size of a Brahman bull. Her eyes widened and her breath caught in her throat. If that rock slipped, it would land squarely on her ankle and every bone in her foot would be crushed.

Her eyes swept the town and the highway leading to the river. Had anyone heard her screams? Surely help would be coming. But no cars moved down the highway from the town. She looked upward, hoping a passing rancher had heard her shouts. No one was in sight.

Moaning, she tried to ease her foot from its precarious position beneath the boulder. Janet winced at the pain. She closed her eyes and steeled herself to make another effort to move it. But it was futile. There was no way to move her foot. It was trapped. She bit her lip to hold back the tears of pain and frustration welling into her eyes and tried to calm herself. Surely someone would find her soon. They had to, she thought desperately, and raised her voice to shout for help.

osity was also returning. She spent several minutes watching Jason stare out the window before she framed the question that was in her mind. "Why did you come looking for me?"

He started at her voice and turned. "I thought you were asleep. It's not even five in the afternoon. You haven't slept four hours."

"I'll sleep later," she assured him. "Why did you search for me? I assume you were looking when you found me."

"Your neighbor called when you didn't come home one night. I told her I doubted there was anything to worry about," he said without looking back at her.

"Do you mean while I was stranded out on a cliff you didn't even look for me? Why did you think there was no need to worry?" she asked, clasping her hands in agitation as she spoke.

Jason's look was penetrating when he turned back to her. "Surely you aren't that innocent. Ron Leonard does stay in a motel in Alva and—" He broke off and then continued calmly. "Anyway, I discovered you weren't with him so I began to search. Luckily your neighbor knew that you often walked along the river."

"I see. So you rescued me like a knight on a white charger." She raised herself in bed as she spoke, and he crossed to stand by the side of her bed.

He gave a deprecating laugh. "You are the type of woman who would see her rescuer as a man on a steed. I can assure you I'm not the storybook hero type." He put a finger in a wispy curl by her face and touched the lock thoughtfully. "I am, however, a

ing, Jason was bending over her bed. "Can you eat this?" he asked as he slipped a hand around her back and raised her gently on the bed.

His new concern was gratifying, but it was also a little embarrassing, she considered. There was no reason for him to treat her like an invalid. "Of course I can," she replied. Her voice did not carry quite as much spirit as she had intended. Jason must have noticed that also for he kept his arm around her as she took the bowl of soup he held out to her. "I can sit up in bed by myself," she said with determination.

"I'm positive you can," he agreed maddeningly, "I'm sure you can also do heavy construction work. However, I don't want to have to clean up the mess if you spill soup all over the bed. I am staying right here beside you to make sure you don't."

It was useless to argue with him, Janet realized. Obediently, she took a sip of the soup and then another before she handed the bowl back to him. "That's all I want."

He replied in a firm voice. "It is hot now and it will be cold later. You're going to eat it before it cools if I have to pour it down your throat."

He had quite a bedside manner, Janet reflected as she took the bowl back and continued to eat. Jason waited by her side until she had finished the last of it.

"Good," he said in satisfaction. "You can go back to sleep now."

"Thank you." The irony she had intended was not even reflected in her voice, Janet thought dispassionately as she lay wearily back on the bed. She was asleep again before she finished her next thought.

When she awoke later, she felt stronger. Her curi-

She watched him as his eyes took in her disheveled hair and slender body outlined beneath the cover.

"Where are my clothes?" she asked.

He shrugged. "Across the room on the table. Are you going to go get them?" Laughter crept into his voice.

The distance across the room looked like a mile to Janet. She didn't think she could have traversed it even if she had wanted to. "Why don't you get them for me?" she whispered hoarsely.

"I don't know," he mused, "I was looking forward to watching you dash over to them. Why don't you just leave your clothes off? I thought," he added, stretching forward a long arm to catch a tendril curl and loop it around his finger, "the look on your face while you watched me sleep meant that I could expect a little repayment for my trouble. I did spend a hell of a long time looking for you and—" Jason broke off abruptly. His expression changed to one of concern. "Why, you're barely able to hold your head up." Surprise was reflected in his words as he made a close study of her face.

"I'm okay," she murmured. "Just take me back to my house."

"Like hell," he returned sharply. "I'm not letting you go anywhere in this condition." As he spoke, he rose and crossed the room. "I'm leaving, but I don't want you to stir from the bed until I get back."

Janet sunk back limply onto the pillow. She wasn't even sure she could have gotten up if she had wanted to. At any rate, he was gone before she could frame a reply. She stared at the rough beamed ceiling for a moment and then her eyelids drifted downward.

When she opened them again at someone's nudg-

bed and lay rigidly. Sleep came to her by degrees. And as she drifted into it she thought of the man who had rescued her from her perch on a cliff. How had he found her? How had he removed her from beneath that rock? And how was she ever going to have the grace to thank him?

By the time she awoke again Janet had had her fill of sleep. It was very early in the morning, she could tell that by the dusky hue of the room. Holding the cover high on her throat to cover her nakedness she leaned forward to look at the man whose back faced her.

She bent over him, holding her breath, not wanting to disturb him until she had explored every contour of his face. As she studied it, her own face softened. He looked curiously peaceful in slumber. Gone was the hard man with the arrogant self-assurance and in his place was this sleeping person who seemed almost like a child, a slight angelic smile curving his hard lips upward. She wanted to touch a lock of his hair, just where it curled a little at the temple, but she didn't dare.

"Do you like what you see?" he asked, his eyes never opening.

Janet started, hugging the cover closer to her as she moved backward away from him. He rolled over with the suppressed strength of a lazy mountain cat and faced her.

"I didn't know you were awake," she said uncertainly. She still felt weak and limp; she knew she wasn't up to sparring with him.

"So I figured," he drawled, propping his head in his hand as he lay on his side and studied her with a trace of scorn.

"Stop it!" Janet cried, tossing her head on the rough mattress in anguish.

He gave a sound of disgust. "If those things bother you, why were you out there to begin with?"

Janet made no answer. The large lump in her throat would have prevented it even if she had wanted to speak.

"There's no use in me sitting up all night," he growled. With those words Jason lifted one long leg and swung himself into bed with her.

"W-What are you doing?" Talking was becoming harder; the words were sticking in her throat.

"I'm going to sleep," he replied.

Janet was dimly aware that she was nude. She didn't want him in bed with her. "You can't get in here. I'm not dressed." She framed the words with difficulty. It was as if there were cotton in her mouth.

"I don't think anyone will be seeing you so you don't have to worry about being fancy," he quipped.

"That's not what I meant. You could . . .," she hesitated and passed her tongue over her dry lips, "Do any number of things," she finished weakly. Her mind was clouding as she spoke.

"Such as?" he asked with interest, lying on his back and staring upward, taking no apparent interest in her body.

She made no answer.

"Don't worry, Miss Prim & Proper. I assure you you don't have a thing to worry about from me. If you could have seen yourself today, you could understand why. All white and limp like that and with one leg swollen like a balloon you are hardly what I would describe as irresistible. Now go to sleep."

Mortified, Janet pulled herself to the edge of the

bed with a mixture of curiosity and anxiety. Who was he?

"Are you awake?" he demanded brusquely, stopping at the bedside.

"Jason?" she asked hesistantly.

"I'm sorry to say that it is. I know you were hoping for someone else, but I suppose helpless people can't be too choosy in selecting a rescuer."

"I fell on the cliff . . . climbing by the river . . . coyotes . . . howling and stalking in the night," she told him in disjointed phrases.

"I'm sure there were coyotes," he told her mercilessly. "You should be glad there was nothing worse. Alabaster Caverns isn't far from there and thousands of bats fly out of it every night to feed, sweeping across the prairie like a dark horde."

"Why are you telling me that?" Janet moaned, shuddering at the thought his words evoked. "I hurt my leg," she told him in a weak appeal for sympathy.

"You're lucky you didn't break your fool neck," he said harshly. "It would have served you right."

Janet shrank back against the mattress at the savageness of his words. She was not able to fight him, not now. She felt so terribly exhausted.

"Only a fool would have tried to climb those rocks," he raged. "What in the hell were you thinking about?"

"I wanted to see the view from the top of them . . ." she began limply and then broke off.

"You can drive to the top," he told her caustically. "Besides the danger of falling there is also the danger of rattlesnakes. They abound in the rocks around the river as do black widow spiders and scorpions."

What was she wearing now? she wondered with a mild curiosity. Again the man's sure hands returned and took from her what little clothing remained, her bikini panties and her stretch bra. Wasn't she naked now? She gave up the effort of trying to determine if she was or not. She just wanted him to go away and leave her alone.

"Go away," she mumbled, but it sounded indistinguishable even to her own ears.

She heard a short laugh, but he ignored her command. Instead he towel-dried her body, moving her this way and that to accomplish his task. Finally he slid a cover over her and she heard his boots thud away. Good, she thought with satisfaction, she could sleep in peace.

It felt like hours later when Janet awoke again. She opened her eyes slowly into pitch blackness. Staring intently into the unrevealing darkness a few forms slowly began to take focus. Wasn't that a stove in one corner of the room? And she could see a table and two chairs near it. Her eyes moved across the tiny room and halted with a stab of apprehension at a chair. A man was sitting it it, his outline tall and powerful.

Events of the last two days came back to her in jumbled pieces. She had gone for a walk along the river and had become trapped on a ledge. She remembered spending a whole miserable day there. What had happened then? She forced herself to recall the scattered details that came vaguely to mind. Someone had carried her from the cliff and brought her to this room. She stirred on the bed and the man rose from the chair. She watched him approach the

moving. Were the rocks sliding again? she wondered vaguely. It didn't seem like it; this was a gentle, swaying motion as if she were on a boat or being carried in someone's arms. That was it! She was being rescued!

Her eyes fluttered open to see a man's western shirt, silver snaps glistening in the sun. It was day again and someone had found her.

"Ron?" she murmured, her eyes falling closed.

"Be quiet," the man ordered shortly.

Was that Ron? It must be because the voice sounded familiar. The swaying motion continued for a time and then she felt a brisker movement as if she were being bounced into the air like a small child—or riding a horse. She smiled groggily to herself. It didn't matter. Someone was taking care of her and there would be no coyotes tonight. She relaxed back to sleep.

Her next consciousness was to feel herself being deposited on something soft. It wasn't rocks, she noted thankfully. It felt like a bed, but of a different texture than she was used to, perhaps a tick mattress. She didn't care. She wanted only to sink back into blissful slumber.

But whoever her rescuer was he would not leave her alone. As she protested with a limp hand upraised, he rolled her around on the bed, pulling off her jacket and then raising her up to draw her knit top over her head. Janet opened her eyes to see the man's back before they fluttered closed again. Was that Ron? It looked too tall to be him. The man must have turned back to her because she could feel him unfastening her jean's zipper and then sliding her pants off.

The coyote howled again and the hair at the base of her scalp tingled with the primitive sound. She cringed. Would the coyotes harm her? Were there wolves in the area? she wondered in fear. She balled her hand into an impotent fist of rage and despair and beat it against the rock, feeling the hard sandstone cut at her hand.

Subsiding weakly back into her sleeping position she willed herself to slip quietly into a sleep that would remove her from her present punishing misery. Gradually she edged back into a trancelike slumber

When she awoke again, she felt a tickling sensation on her neck. She fluttered her hand behind her head, swatting absently, and the tickling touched her hand. Rain, she realized in dismay, was setting in with a steady drizzle.

"Oh no," she breathed aloud.

But her denial was in vain. The sky opened and sent forth a drenching stream of water. It lasted only a short time, but the effect was devastating to Janet. She buried her face in her hands and cried helplessly.

In despair she began to fear for her life. What if no one found her? No one ever came out to these cliffs except her. If anyone did, she had never seen them. How long, then, would it be before she was missed?

At that thought Janet reassured herself. Ron stopped by nearly every day. Surely he would look for her if she was gone. And Bessie would notice after a day or so. Janet offered a prayer that a search for her was already underway and lapsed slowly into a stuporlike sleep.

The next time Janet awakened it was to feel herself

CHAPTER 8

Janet awoke from her half-sleep to hear a spine-tingling wail. Terrified, she looked down at the moonlit valley below to see two shadowy, doglike creatures walking across the pastureland on the other side of the river. The animal dirge was repeated as one of the creatures raised its glittering eyes heavenward and formed the melancholy sound deep in its throat.

Coyotes. Janet stiffened at the sound of them. Around her the night air was chilly, seeping through her light jacket with a coolness that chilled her skin and clutched at her bones. Shifting positions, she tried not to think of the cold. Her head rested uncomfortably on the giant boulder that imprisoned her. She felt the full misery of having lain helpless for nearly eighteen hours. At least she thought it must be that long. Her watch had been smashed and no longer worked, but the day had come and gone and it was now well into the night.

Her attempts to summon help during the day had become increasingly more feeble and she had felt her strength waning. Now—cold, hungry, and frightened—the weight of her problems surrounded her as certainly as the thick night air.

man who appreciates an attractive woman and you are that."

She watched Jason seat himself on the side of the bed. Then he bent to kiss her. She did not return his kisses immediately, but she did not push him away. His lips invaded hers more deeply and a pleasant stirring sent a blanket of warmth through her. Slowly, she put her arms around his neck and clung to him.

He had looked for her. He had shown real concern where she would not have expected any from him. She was grateful. If it had not been for him, she still might be trapped on the bluff.

There was more to her response than gratitude. Naked under the cover that separated them, Janet felt her body come alive with a thirst for Jason that was more powerful than any emotion she had felt before. As his mouth explored hers it seemed to Janet that the sky was turning more and more golden as the sun mounted in the sky. Within herself her own sun was rising also, making her feel warm and glowing and vibrantly alive. A pulse throbbed wildly in her throat and her breath was stopped in it. The physical signs of her desire were nothing compared with her emotional turmoil. She felt as if an earthquake were erupting within and the liquid lava spilling down the mountainside was melting her in its consuming heat.

Still his lips demanded more and his body pressed against hers, with a persistence that proclaimed he wanted even more intimate contact with her than they now shared. And Janet concurred with his feelings. She longed to share with him the fire that burned within her and to give him some of the radiant warmth that engulfed her.

In a swirl of feeling Janet was conscious of the sensuous nearness of the lean length of his body, the catch of his breathing, and the potent yearning of her own body for his. Still her lips clung to his and still he pressed himself closer to her.

Then Jason slid a hand beneath the cover, moving steadily toward the firm mound of her heaving breast. She felt his sure hand close around one swell, cupping it, and she breathed a sigh of pure contentment.

She was floating, faster and faster, being swept away on a current that went down the river at a breathtaking speed and ended she knew not where. A picture of a rushing river came into her mind, swirling around rapids and hurtling over falls, beyond its own control, pushed relentlessly forward by its own power. The river had lost control of its own destiny in the same way she had. And she didn't care.

But something inside her did care. A small but insistent voice cried out to be heard as she trembled to Jason's touch and felt the sweet warmth of his mouth on hers. She was letting things go entirely beyond her control and soon she would find herself crashing over a falls, awakening at the bottom to discover herself washed out of the river, abandoned and alone. The thought gave her pause. In the midst of her enjoyment there was a coloring of uneasiness. She was only another woman to Jason and she would be cast aside once he had what he wanted.

Janet stirred in his arms, lifting her hand from around his neck and pushing his stroking hand away from her breast. He swept her hand aside and continued his slow, erotic exploration.

His lips left her mouth by a fraction and when he spoke, his breath went into her body and she could feel the soft movement of his lips against hers.

"Jason, wait."

"Why are you fighting something we both want?" he asked roughly.

Janet felt an inner fire kindle. She did want him, she admitted truthfully, but not like this—not as an object and as someone for whom Jason felt no affection. Who knew where he had passed his other nights? She was just one more woman to him. There had to be something stronger before she could give herself to him.

"I can't."

"Why not?" he taunted. "Because you are a faithful woman and you wouldn't betray Ron? You're just like any other woman. You already have betrayed him with your kisses and your desire for me."

"Ron doesn't have anything to do with this."

"No," he agreed callously, "he probably doesn't. The fact that you spend every waking moment with him shouldn't instill any sense of loyalty in you for him. It really doesn't matter if the man is in love with you. To you he's just another toy to play with for a time and then discard."

"You don't know me at all." Janet looked directly into his cold blue eyes.

He swung himself off the bed, towering over her as he put his hands on his hips and stood with legs astride. "I know you well enough. And I know your type. Oh, you play at being sweet and caring, but all the time you want to lure a man into your silken web and then sting him to death."

"I certainly didn't try to lure you!" she retorted.

"No? I think you did. For a time I thought I might have misjudged you, but I didn't. You're just like all the others."

"Yes," Janet retorted, goaded, "I am the same. I have Ron on the string and I want you and who knows what man I will set my trap for after that? While you," she hissed, "are the most faithful of men. Georgia can sleep soundly in the knowledge that you would never try to pick up another woman because you are so devoted to her."

"Georgia has been around; she knows the score. Besides," he added roughly, "I don't have to explain my actions to you."

"You bet your life you don't," Janet threw at him, ice in her voice, "and I'm sure not going to explain mine to you. Now bring my clothes over here and get out."

"At your service," he said with mock humility. He stalked across to the table and picked up her bundle of clothes. Returning, he dropped them on the bed without looking at her, turned on his heel, and stalked from the room.

It was just as well he hadn't looked at her, Janet consoled herself, because tears of rage stood in her eyes and she wouldn't give him the satisfaction of thinking he had made her cry.

Ten minutes later she was dressed and limping painfully to the door. Her ankle, forgotten for a time in the emotion of the moment, was throbbing now that she had put her weight on it. She hobbled out the door and looked around. In the distance she could see the Stewart Spanish-style home, majestic atop a hill. She looked at the rough-hewn building near her. It must be the cabin Susan had pointed out to her.

"Are you ready?" Jason demanded, coming up beside her.

"Why did you bring me here instead of taking me to the house?"

"If you think I intended to seduce you, you overestimate your charm. If I'd gone riding up to the house bearing your broken body, there would have been a hell of a lot of questions. You can field your own questions."

"What did you tell Bessie?"

His eyes shifted off to the distance. "I told her you were spending a day or so with Susan."

"Why do you think I would want to hide my mistake?" she asked, drawing herself up proudly. "I realize now it was stupid to attempt to climb the bluff, but I am certainly willing to admit my error. I," she finished with a cool look at him, "do not think myself so perfect that I won't admit my faults."

"Really? How noble," he sneered. "If you are quite through with your little lecture, perhaps you would consent to mount this horse so that we may be on our way."

"I can't ride that animal," Janet protested, looking at the large beast tied to a railing by the side of the cabin. "I don't ride."

"Don't worry. I ride *quite* well and I will be on the horse with you."

"I'm not going with you," she declared with finality. She could hear the petulance in her voice and was annoyed with herself. It was not a matter worth arguing, she knew, but she stood firm. She didn't want him close to her, she resented him ordering her around, and finally, she was in a foul humor this morning and he was only making it worse.

"Miss Matthews." His patience was worn thin and his voice grated, "I dislike arguing with you over every damn thing. Couldn't you close your mouth for five seconds and listen to reason? I brought you here on my horse and I am taking you back to the ranch on it and that's that." With those words he advanced steadily toward her, his body agile as a stalking mountain lion. He reached her and gathered her roughly into his arms.

As he swung her off her feet, Janet realized it was pointless to protest. And she was losing both the physical and emotional ability to fight. The strength she had awakened with had been of short duration. Now it was deserting her like a faithless friend, leaving her weak once again.

A moment later she was deposited unceremoniously on Jason's horse. He sprang onto the saddle behind her and looked past her as he cantered the horse across the gently rolling pastureland toward the house.

A few minutes later he pulled the animal up short in front of the house. "The rest of the ride won't be nearly so exciting, ma'am," he drawled in an exaggerated version of a cowboy's speech. "We'll take m'ah car."

She said nothing as she waited for him to dismount and help her from the horse. He slid down and held his hands up for her. Then he swung her off the mount and placed her on the ground in front of him.

"Thank you," she whispered. The earth was beginning to spin under her feet. Even though she was trying to keep the weight off her injured leg, a persistent throb ached there and she winced at the pain.

Jason must have seen her look for he lifted her with an easy movement and carried her into the house. She didn't even protest until he had deposited her on the couch in the living room and stepped back.

"You can take me home now," she murmured in a hoarse voice. She wanted to get out of his house as quickly as possible. "I feel well enough to travel," she added when he made no reply to her statement.

"I'm calling a doctor," he informed her brusquely. "The swelling in your foot is causing you more pain than I had expected. You're not leaving this house until I am sure you're all right."

Janet might have been more appreciative of his words had they been uttered in a more gentle tone. As it was, she felt like a horse with a broken leg—useless and in the way. But he was right about one thing: her leg was causing her pain. Since she didn't think she could move much anyway, she lay quietly on the couch while he crossed to the phone and picked it up.

Closing her eyes, she listened to him speaking into the receiver. Then he hung up and came back to her. "The doctor's going to stop by on his way home. It's six o'clock now so he'll be here shortly."

"Thank you," she replied in as gracious a voice as she could muster. She closed her eyes again, deliberately shutting Jason out of her consciousness.

The doctor did come later. He wrapped her leg in strong bandages and briskly told her there was no reason not to walk on it. In fact, he insisted she begin to move around.

"She's stayed off of it because it's causing her pain," Jason explained to the white-haired man as the doctor closed his bag and rose.

"Course it is," the old man snapped. "Anyone who does a fool thing like climbing the cliffs near the river should expect what they get. Damn lucky thing she's alive after that slide." He glared at Janet. "I'll show myself out."

Janet looked up at Jason after the doctor left. "Does it gratify you to have the good physician echo your sentiments about my intelligence?" she asked tartly.

"Getting your spirit back, I see," he said blandly. "Don't look so piqued, you know what he said was true. Now," he continued briskly. "I have a couple of things to do and then I'll take you home." He turned and walked out of the room.

Janet was just attempting to put the doctor's orders into practice and rise from the couch when Susan burst through the front door. A welcoming smile lit her small face as she saw Janet. "I didn't know you were here. Your car isn't outside," she said breathlessly.

"Your uncle brought me," Janet explained briefly.

"Oh," Susan said. With a child's abruptness, she changed the subject. "Come on back to my bedroom. I'll show you the new curtains and bedspread I've picked out of the catalog."

Janet limped down the hall after her. Susan didn't even notice her teacher's disability as she scurried into her room and left the door open for Janet to follow. "Are you redoing your room?" Janet asked as she stepped inside the little girl's bland green room with its flowered spread on the bed. A picture of a matador over the bed completed the motel effect Janet had noted the last time she was here.

"No," Susan admitted slowly. "But I was pretending.

"I see," Janet murmured and sat down on the floor beside Susan, exclaiming with her over the pictures of frilly eyelet bedspreads and curtains and concurring with Susan's lavish praise of a room decorated in girlish pink with lacey ruffles.

An hour later a knock sounded on Susan's door and Jason opened the door. He glanced at the open catalog on the floor. "I'm ready to go now, Miss Matthews. Did you eat anything?"

She disregarded his question. "Susan was just showing me some lovely pictures of little girls' rooms in the catalog," Janet began, "I think it would be very nice if she could redo her own room to make it look more homey."

His eyes rested on her face for an instant, impassively. "Do you?" He turned and walked from the room.

Janet rose stiffly, nursing her sprained leg as she limped down the hall after him. Susan followed them out the front door.

"Can I go with you?" she asked, reaching the car and standing wistfully beside it as Janet maneuvered herself into the front seat, easing in her injured leg.

"No," Jason said shortly. He slammed his car door. Janet barely had time to wave to Susan and call a fleeting good-bye before he started the engine. Then he spun the car around and headed it down the road. Janet tilted her chin up and focused her eyes resolutely out the side window, willing herself not to look at him.

They drove the whole distance back to Freedom in silence. It was a silence fraught with unspoken hostility. He pulled up in front of her house and stopped the motor. "Do you need any help?" he asked indifferently as she opened the door and eased herself laboriously out.

She whirled to face him. "Thank you, no, Mr. Stewart." Her words were short and succinct. On an impulse, she added, "You'll be glad to know that I may be leaving town to take a teaching position elsewhere."

The look that passed over his face was one of surprise coupled with dissatisfaction, but he said nothing.

"Does that make you happy?" she pressed.

"Turning tail and running? What exactly is it that you are afraid of?"

"Certainly not you," she returned smugly.

"Did I suggest it was me?" he asked tersely.

"No, but you think it is," she countered. "I'll admit that your threat to have me fired did start me looking for a job in Tulsa."

"Tulsa," he rolled the word across his tongue. "Isn't that where Ron lives?"

"Yes."

"How nice. So now you are going to go back to being a faithful girlfriend to him. Such loyalty," he commented sarcastically. He started the engine and leaned across to pull her door closed. Then he drove off, leaving her to limp unassisted inside.

Janet turned and walked slowly to her house. Within, all was peaceful and serene, just as she had left it. The geraniums in the window box were blooming cheerful reds and pinks. Nothing within the house gave any signs that the mistress had walked out two days earlier to be trapped on a cliff's edge.

She limped into the bedroom and continued on through to the bathroom, giving only the most wistful of glances at the bed. Later she could rest and take the weight off her foot. Now she needed to take a nice relaxing bath.

The phone's ring distracted her from her task just as she was laying out the towels. She set them on the side of the old pedestal lavatory and went to answer it.

"Hello," she said.

"Hi, how are you?"

"I'm fine, Ron." She didn't feel up to going into a dissertation of the events of the last few days. It was simpler to tell a harmless lie.

"Good. I ran into your neighbor and she told me you were spending a couple of days visiting Jason's niece. You didn't tell me you were going to be gone," he chided mildly.

"I didn't plan on it," she said truthfully. "It just sort of happened."

"I understand. Did you have a nice time?"

"Yes," she replied, easing herself onto the couch as she spoke and wincing at the pain.

"I'm glad you enjoyed yourself. Would you like to go to a movie this weekend?"

"Sounds fine," she replied, leaning down to massage her throbbing foot.

"I'll call you back after I find out what's playing. Bye."

Janet hung up the phone and stared down at it. She was back home. Ron was calling and everything had returned to normal. Jason was out of her life again. All that remained was to put him from her thoughts.

CHAPTER 9

"Going to be hot for the rodeo," Bessie predicted, looking at the sky with one hand shading her eyes.

"I hope it's not too hot," Janet replied.

"I've seen it when it was over one-hundred degrees and folks still flocked into town, same as they're doing now."

Janet looked down their quiet street to where it terminated at the spur highway leading off from the main road that connected Alva to Woodward. Ordinarily there was little or no traffic on the highway, but today pickup followed pickup, all coming to town for tomorrow's rodeo.

"I guess you're going to the dance after the rodeo," Bessie said.

"Yes, Ron's taking me."

"Well, hope you have a good time," Bessie noted, ending their conversation as she turned to go back into her house.

"I will," Janet predicted merrily. She would too. For an Indiana girl who had never heard of the two step eight months ago, she felt pure country and western now. She was going to go to the dance tomorrow and her feet were already itching at the thought of it. It had been ages since she had really kicked up her heels.

Yesterday she had made a special trip all the way to Enid to pick out just the right dress for the dance. After trying on some long peasant skirts and a few chic pairs of designer jeans, she had finally happened onto the perfect dress in a little out of the way shop. It was a sundress with spaghetti straps. With its white cotton background and cheerful sprinkling of red poppies across the hem and bustline it showed off her deep tan to perfection. She had even bought a little artificial nosegay of red flowers to put in her hair and new white sandals. The rodeo was a matter of indifference to her, but she could hardly wait for the dance.

When Ron picked her up the next day, she looked like half of the girls in the now-crowded town. A pair of jeans was molded to her slender hips and a green and white checked shirt was tucked into them. She even had a western hat of loosely woven straw and a pair of leather boots.

"You look like a real cowgirl," Ron greeted her with a grin, looking western himself in an outfit similar to hers, but with a blue plaid shirt.

"Thanks, I feel like a barrel racer," she laughed.

"We better go now if we want to get good seats."

Janet picked up her clutch purse and followed him out the door. They walked the four blocks to the rodeo, threading their way through traffic as they crossed the busy road to the rodeo arena. Inside the arena Ron took her hand and steered her through the crowd to a good pair of seats near the top of the bleachers.

"How's this?" he asked.

"Fine."

Janet looked around herself for people she knew as she seated herself. Freedom, dead for a good part of the year, came alive for the biggest event of every summer, the rodeo. And people who had not been back to their home town all year came for this annual rite. As she glanced around she saw some of her students with their parents as well as some grocery store acquaintances with their families.

"Everyone certainly is here, aren't they? They must have come from miles."

"Yeah, they come from all over. This is darn near as big an event as the cow chip throwing contest at Beaver."

"Cow chip?" she looked at him questioningly.

Ron laughed. "What's a nice way to put it?" he asked himself. "Cow chips are dried pieces of cow manure."

"They really throw them?" Janet asked in disbelief.

"They sure do."

Their conversation was interrupted by the first strains of music coming over the loudspeaker and everyone stood, stetsons and ten-gallon hats coming off for the national anthem. At the last strains of the song, the crowd gave a rousing cheer and the rodeo was on. Janet watched in fascination as girls raced expertly trained horses around barrels. After that teams of men roped goats and then daredevils on bucking broncos catapulted out of the stalls and clung on bravely.

"They must be crazy," Janet whispered to Ron.

"You think they're crazy, wait until you see the wild bull riders."

As the rodeo continued Janet realized that Bessie's prediction had been right. It *was* hot. And as the mid-August sun crept higher in the sky it became hotter, turning into a real scorcher of a day. She looked around to see people in the crowd fanning themselves with their programs. Glancing back at the pageantry still taking place before her Janet saw clowns dancing around trying to distract a bull. Her interest in the all-American sport was lagging. She looked around at the spectators again.

Suddenly her eyes stopped. Four rows ahead of her a blond woman, wearing a wide-brimmed Scarlett O'Hara hat, was snuggling close to the tall man beside her. Even from the back Janet could tell who the man was. The square, firm set of his shoulders was unmistakable. And when the woman straightened and he turned to say something to her, his rugged profile clearly verified what Janet already suspected. It was Jason Stewart.

So Jason was still seeing Georgia? Her heart sank. She didn't know why she would have thought they weren't still a couple. But the knowledge that they were was somehow disheartening.

"Did you see that?" Ron demanded as the crowd went wild, yelling and waving their hats.

"No," she admitted as she rose to her feet alongside the other spectators. Through the hats and heads she could only vaguely see what looked like an expert rider, clinging to a bucking bull with one hand as if he were riding a hobby horse.

"What a rider!"

"Yes, he's good," Janet agreed as the crowd subsided back into their seats while the man slid from the back of the bull and picked up his hat from the dust.

Janet's mind wandered away from the rodeo again and back to the scene taking place in front of her. Georgia appeared to have no more interest in the sport than did Janet. She was tapping Jason's arm playfully. He did not turn to look at her, which gave Janet a curious sense of satisfaction.

"Well, it's over," Ron announced, standing.

"It is?" Janet asked.

"Yes. I guess we'd better be getting back and clean up for tonight. I'll have to drive back to the motel to change, but that'll give you time to change and eat something. They'll have food at the dance hall, but it might be good to grab a bite of something first. Tonight there will be more drinking than eating."

She and Ron made their way through the mass of people heading back toward their cars and trucks. Breaking free of the crowd they walked down the side street to Janet's house.

"I won't come in," Ron said as he stopped at his brown car parked in front of her house. " 'I'll be back in an hour and a half. See you then."

"Bye," Janet called, walking down the sidewalk to her door and stepping inside to the air-conditioned comfort of the house.

She turned on the water in the bathtub and plugged in her electric rollers before laying out the items she would wear tonight.

Holding the new dress up in front of herself she smiled. It was a lovely dress and she was going to be lovely tonight too. She was going to dance every dance, smiling and flirting to her heart's content. Three weeks from now she would be in Tulsa, hunting an apartment and leaving the half-wild West behind.

Her spirits flagged at the prospect of her move. She had accepted the job that was offered after considerable prompting from Ron. But reservations about going and reasons not to go had been cropping up daily. She pushed the thought of leaving firmly from her mind. Tonight was for fun; she wasn't going to let any unpleasant thoughts intrude. Walking to the bathroom she pulled off her jeans, shirt, and underclothes and stepped into the tepid bath, sprinkling bubble bath in belatedly and frothing up the water with her hands.

Ten minutes later she stepped out of the tub, clean and refreshed. She toweled dry and put on her new sundress before carefully applying the merest touches of makeup. She added a hint of mascara to her already long, curving lashes and a touch of lip gloss to bring out the sensuous shape of her lips. Then she turned her attention to her hair, catching it back with barrettes above each ear and clipping the red flower at one side. She surveyed herself critically in the mirror. She liked the effect.

A knock sounded on the front door and she started toward it, pulling on her sandals as she went.

"Hi," Ron said as she opened the door. "I'm back a little early. Are you ready?"

"Yes. Do you want to come in?"

"No, let's go on over to the dance hall. There's going to be one heck of a crowd so we might as well get there early."

"Good. I'm dying to dance."

"You look nice," Ron complimented her as they stepped outside the door and started toward the tiny downtown. It was crowded now with people and vehicles, all heading toward the large American Legion hall at one end of the town where the dance was being held.

Ron had been right about going early to avoid the crowd. Unfortunately they were not early enough. The line of people waiting in the street to gain entrance to the noisy hall was growing steadily longer. She and Ron took a place at the end of the line and waited patiently, smiling and talking to other couples, young and old, as they moved toward the door.

From within the building the strains of a pure country band played a snappy beat that set Janet's foot tapping in time. She could hardly wait to get inside and exercise her yearning feet on the dance floor.

It was several minutes more before they were inside the building. Then Janet stepped into the dimly-lit room and gazed around the crowded hall. Couples around the sides of the large room hugged each other, while other pairs kept up a swinging step to the music, swirling around the floor. The men, in their Saturday night clothes consisting of good western-cut pants and checked or plaid shirts, still wore their stetsons and pointed cowboy boots. Their partners were more diversified in their apparel. Some of them were sporting outfits that matched the men's, complete with hat, while others were in more feminine dresses and a few even wore long gowns. The old mingled with the young.

"This is quite a crowd," Janet said, a catch of excitement in her voice.

"It sure is," Ron agreed as he steered her toward

the back wall where a long bar dispensed liquid refreshment. "What do you want to drink?"

"Nothing yet. I want to dance."

Ron laughed. "And you will. I've never seen a girl so anxious to get out on a dance floor and try her legs out." Ron stopped to nod to a group of men he knew and then started out onto the dance floor with her.

Halfway out to the floor, as they were winding their way through the crowd surrounding the dancers, a man stopped Ron. Janet recognized him as one of the men who worked at the rig.

"Sorry, Ron," the man began apologetically, "I hate to bother you, but we have bad problems . . ."

The rest of his words were lost as Janet was jostled away from Ron. But when he joined her a moment later, his words confirmed what she had suspected—he was going to have to leave.

"I don't know how to tell you this, Janet," Ron began, "but I've got to go out to Great Salt Plains Lake to see about the barge drilling they're doing. The geologist over there is sick and they're on a crucial hole."

"But it's nine o'clock at night," she objected.

"I know," he said regretfully, "but they work on the lake at night because the winds are calmer then. I'm really sorry, but I've got to get over there. They won't be through until six in the morning."

"Problems?" a man's voice cut into their discussion.

Janet looked up at the sound of the familiar voice. Jason Stewart was standing right beside her.

"I'm afraid so," Ron told him. "It's nothing serious, but I'll have to take Janet home now and she's been looking forward to this dance for weeks."

"You don't have to take me home," Janet declared.

"I can't leave you here by yourself; it wouldn't be safe."

"Why not? Freedom is the safest town I know. No one would bother me here."

"That's true most of the time, but tonight is different," he explained. "Some of these men haven't been out for a real night on the town in quite some time and they're drinking pretty hard. It wouldn't be wise to let you walk home by yourself in the dark."

"I can take care of Miss Matthews," Jason volunteered with an impassive look at Janet.

Suddenly she was intensely aware of his virility as he towered above the other heads in the crowd, looking lean and capable in his casual clothes. Tonight, heady with the excitement of the dance and buoyed up by the enthusiasm of the people around her, tonight she knew she would not be safe with Jason.

"No," she said hurriedly. "Take me home now, Ron. I wouldn't want to put Mr. Stewart to any trouble. I really don't mind missing the dance."

"Janet," Ron laughed, "you've been looking forward to this for so long. Why, you haven't talked about anything else for days; you'll be very disappointed if I take you home now. If Jason will look after you, then that's good enough for me. I think he could hold his own with any man who tried to give you trouble."

"But Ron," Janet protested. Too late, he had turned and was making his way through the throng toward the door. She turned her gaze slowly back to

Jason, directing her eyes to rest on the second button of his shirt. Above it little tufts of curling dark hair peeped from his shirt and the sight was disconcerting. His forceful male presence was undeniable and alarming. Why had Ron deserted her?

Jason put a light arm around her waist; and she started at the unexpected feel of it.

"Skittish as a young colt, aren't you?" he asked, his voice laden with amusement.

Janet looked up to see the glint of laughter in his cobalt eyes. The hand that had come possessively around to her waist sent tingling sensations up her spine and her lips quivered with the intensity of the feeling.

"There's nothing to be alarmed about," he told her silkily, "I was merely going to make certain I didn't lose you in the crowd."

"I can take care of myself," she returned crisply.

"I'm sure you can," he agreed, "but from the looks men are casting in your direction it might take all your strength. Why don't we join the dancers?"

"No, thank you."

"Why not?"

"Because I don't want to dance," she said levelly.

"Really? Well I do." With those words he drew her toward the floor, edging his way to a cleared space before he stopped and gathered her up into his arms, drawing her head down until it rested on his chest.

The dance, Janet realized belatedly, was a slow one. While the singer crooned, the couples around them moved in slow time to the music, their bodies pressed tightly together. To pull away from Jason, she knew would create a scene. And worse, he would probably yank her right back into his arms. There was nothing to do but finish this dance with him.

"Your moves are a little wooden," Jason commented low to her ear, "but you'll loosen up after six or seven dances."

"This is the only dance I'm going to have with you," she declared. The fact that he made no reply to her statement only annoyed her more. "Did you hear me?"

"I heard you," he said, shifting his body slightly so that she fell gently against him. His arms pulled her closer to him and she could feel his breath fanning her cheek as they danced.

They completed the dance in silence, Janet's resentment against him slowly dissolving under the sensuous movements of his body next to hers. Tonight, she told herself weakly, she would call a brief truce. After this dance was over she would have him take her home. Until he did there was no reason why she shouldn't enjoy herself.

The music ended and Janet felt a prickle of regret as Jason moved away from her. "I want to go home now."

"Why?" he countered, making no move.

"I just do," she maintained. She certainly wasn't going to tell him that she didn't trust herself with him. Jason shrugged. Taking her by the hand she looked up in surprise as he led her through the crowd toward the door. They reached it and stepped outside. In the fuzzy glow of the street light Janet saw men sharing six packs of beer as well as bottles wrapped in brown paper sacks. Jason nodded to them as he led her past them and drew her off the wooden sidewalk and around to the side of the building.

"What are you doing?" she demanded as he put a hand on either side of her, trapping her with her back to the building.

"I just wanted to talk to you."

She avoided his eyes. "I don't want to talk to you." Her breath was coming in heavy puffs and she could feel her heart pounding. The very nearness of him sent a current of excitement through her.

"Janet," he continued as if she had not spoken, "there is no reason we could not have a nice time tonight."

"I don't think we could," she countered. He could be persuasive, she knew, but she had allowed him to intrude into her life once too often; it wouldn't happen tonight.

In the glow from the street she glanced up to see his hard features soften into a smile and unwillingly some of her resistance melted. "Of course we can," he assured her. As he spoke he kept a hand on either side of her, not touching her. But his face came steadily closer until it was only inches from hers. "And let's start the evening off right with a friendly agreement to cease our constant bickering, at least for tonight." He pulled her closer to him, one large hand resting on the swell of her hip while the other played in the curls at her shoulders.

Janet opened her mouth; she didn't know what she intended to say, but his lips settled on her parted ones before she had a chance to speak. And in the magic of the night she brought her hands up to his chest and rested them gently against him, one finger dancing through the tiny chest hairs curling out of his shirt. She would be leaving Freedom soon, surely she could allow herself just this moment to remember Jason by. His mouth touched hers with a provocative sureness and sleeping passions awakened within her. Her hands went up to curve around his neck, drawing him closer to eliminate the very small space that separated their bodies.

Her racing pulse pounded in her ears as yet another sign of the havoc he was creating within, and the roar of it made her think briefly they might be near an ocean instead of landlocked on the Plains. It didn't matter where they were; she was with Jason. Her knees felt weak with the trembling that shook them, sending a a shiver through her.

Slowly Jason released her. "I don't think we should start anything we can't finish," he told her, regret coloring his voice. He gave a soft laugh and his lips came down to brush against her flushed cheek. "Why don't we go back in and enjoy ourselves?" he suggested.

Janet nodded dumbly and let him take her hand and lead her back through the crowd of men outside the door, in the process of starting a brawl among themselves. They parted respectfully and waited to continue the fight until Jason and Janet had passed through the knot.

He held her close by his side as they went back into the dance hall. The loud music blended with the thumping sound of people keeping time with their feet. And the swaying motions of the dancers all combined in Janet's mind with the dizzying kiss she had just enjoyed. She felt lighthearted and happy.

She smiled up at Jason as he swung her onto the floor. They went through the fast steps of a rollicking dance in perfect time with each other. And when he drew her back into his arms for the sweet strains of "San Antonio Rose," it seemed as if the twin Texas fiddles were playing only for her. Snuggling against the smooth fabric of his shirt she matched her steps to his long ones, letting him guide her through the dance he performed with expert smoothness. She closed her eyes and savored the feeling. Tonight was special, she thought with drowsy contentment.

The dance ended. "You're not going to sleep on me, are you?" Jason teased.

"No." She shook her head as she opened her eyes to look into his amazingly blue ones. "No," she repeated in a husky voice, her eyes never leaving his face.

During the hours that followed Janet felt as if she were living out a fantasy. The strong, sure feel of Jason's arms around her gave her a sense of security and comfort she had never experienced before. The smell of him and the touch of the soft cotton shirt where she rested her head against his shoulder conspired to make her feel almost giddy. It was too perfect to be something from reality; this could only be a waking dream.

Finally, as other couples began to trickle from the building and move homeward in the early hours of the morning, Jason took her arm and they strolled wordlessly back to her house. Outside the door she threw her head back and looked up at the stars that were clearly outlined in the black velvet pile of the country sky.

"Everything has been perfect tonight," she murmured.

"Yes."

Jason opened the door for her, following her into the darkened house and reaching for her hand as she felt for the light switch.

"Don't turn the light on," he said as he brought his lips to hers in a hungry kiss.

The hand that had been searching the wall diverted its direction and wrapped itself around Jason's neck. Her fingers moved slowly in the soft hair at the nape of his neck as she gave herself over to his embrace, feeling with a breathless wonder his hands moving with controlled desire, stroking down her body to her hips and then pulling her closer to him. The sure, firm feel of Jason sent a tremor of longing through her and she arched herself against him.

It was like none of the other kisses they had ever shared before. She wanted him totally and she knew that tonight would be the moment when the slow burning fires that had been smoldering within her for so long would be fanned to life, and she would be consumed in the blaze.

His mouth probed hers hungrily and she felt a feverish ache for him that was so strong it left her feeling weak and trembling, clinging to Jason like a drowning person clinging to a raft. His lips left hers to nuzzle at her ear before moving downward to the base of her throat.

Then he picked her up and swung her into his arms, carrying her easily through the darkened house into the bedroom and finding the bed with the aid of the dim light filtering in from the window. He laid her down on top the covers and followed her down onto the bed, his lips and hands becoming more insistent, almost urgent, as they moved across her body.

In a matter of minutes he had divested her of her clothes and she watched from the bed as he stood and stripped himself—the tall silhouette of him framed against the lace-curtained window. She could not draw her eyes from the hypnotic sight of his naked torso as he advanced to the bed and moved down onto it. She reached out a hand and touched the hard flesh of his shoulders, burying her head against it as he began a sure voyage of discovery over her body, unmasking areas of aching tenderness that she had not known she possessed.

Every nerve in her body responded to the intoxicating sensation of his touch, and the dormant emotions within her churned like the boiling lava within a volcano.

And through the fog of her own aroused senses she was blissfully aware of Jason's own heightened passions. The erratic tattoo of his heartbeat told her that he was as alive with the feel of her as she was with the touch of him. And his thickened breathing against her ear as his tongue stroked the ultrasensitive skin of her earlobe told her more plainly than words that he desired her.

Her hands moved downward to stroke his strong back and then lower to caress his naked thighs. He gave a groan at her touch and his lips came back to hers with bruising force. And while her own lips answered his unreservedly, thrilling to the feel of his tongue darting into her mouth, she was trembling with the sensations she felt as he caressed the hidden valleys of her body. Her hands moved against the smooth skin of his body, savoring the feel of it as she reveled in the primitive joy his hands were evoking.

He dragged his mouth away from hers, down to

the pillar of her neck. He kissed the hollow of it before descending lower to her breasts and settling on one pointed peak, running his tongue over it in tantalizing circular motions.

She moaned softly with pleasure, moving her head restlessly on the pillow and closing her eyes against the exquisite pressure of his hands. His mouth returned to hers, ravaging against her own passion-swollen lips with an intensity that vaguely surprised her, even in the unsteady excitement of the moment.

And then he began to move her, placing her just so on the bed. His lips never left hers as he turned her to meet his body. His face was intent as he brought them together and she knew he was taking time to go slowly and gently. His body began to rock against her, gradually involving her in the motion. His lips came back to seal hers and her eyes fluttered closed.

She felt a great calmness interrupted only now and again by the undefinable, nameless sensation that coursed through her. And then the feeling became more steady and increased in timbre, building again on the sea like another crashing wave, but this time one of infinite delight.

The hard pounding of his heart was as exciting to her as the ragged "Janet," that he murmured into her ear. She gave a breaking sob and dug her nails tighter into his thighs as he brought them even closer together. And then he moved again and this time she knew she was lost.

She cried out with uncontrolled passion. The wonder of this strange new feeling was almost as unbearable as the sheer, boundless ecstasy of it. Her breathing was out of control—as if it were being driven out of her by a strong gale. And her eyes, even tightly closed, still saw lights in vivid colors she had never seen before. And with her, sharing the moment in a way that she could feel in every pore, was Jason.

When they finally subsided together on the bed, their bodies drifting apart, she felt an incomprehensible sense of fulfillment that not even the parting of their bodies could erase. She had given herself totally to Jason. What she had given to him could only have been bestowed to a man who was more special to her than any other man would ever be. And as she reached out to stroke the curve of his cheek, feeling a light film of perspiration on it, she knew that she had no regrets. She loved Jason as she would never love any other man. Her lips curved upward at that thought and she drifted off to sleep in perfect contentment.

When she awoke the following morning, she fluttered her eyelashes open and stretched like a purring kitten, turning toward Jason. She blinked in surprise as she saw that the space beside her was empty. He was gone. An ache of disappointment throbbed in her throat.

She reached down and picked up the clock ticking beside her bed. Ten o'clock. Of course he was gone. Jason was a man with a ranch to run, she reminded herself, and he could not stay here indefinitely. Oh, but if he could! She closed her eyes again and savored the memory of last night.

The phone sounded in the living room. Janet made no move to rise to answer it. Intruders. She wanted no one bursting in upon her thoughts today. She wanted only to relive endlessly the lovely night that had been.

She finally rose and pulled on her white shorts and a bright green striped blouse. She brushed her hair, smiling at herself in the mirror as she did so. Her hair was growing longer now, inches past her shoulders, and a little of the whimsical curl from last night still lingered. The sun had streaked it an interesting color of light and dark red, and cleaned and brushed as it was now it had the shine of a penny being twirled in the sunlight. And her skin had also taken on the golden hue of a sun worshiper. But the glow in her cheeks and the sparkle in her clear brown eyes—she laughed conspiratorially at her reflection—she knew where those had come from. That afternoon, after a brisk walk by the river and a pleasant hour spent tending her plants, the telephone sounded again. This time she walked to the living room and answered it, one hand still wearing a cotton glove and holding her small trowel.

"Hello."

"Hi," Ron greeted her, "did you have a good time last night?"

"Yes," she told him slowly. She felt a moment of guilt as she considered what had happened last night from Ron's standpoint.

"Good. I saw Jason today and he said he really didn't mind taking care of you at all."

"Is that all he said?" she asked casually.

"Well," he laughed, "promise you won't tell him I told you so because he asked me to keep this a secret, but Jason is planning on getting married. He wasn't sure about the date but I imagine that's something he and Georgia will soon set."

Janet felt herself go cold, the trowel slipped from

her nerveless fingers and thudded onto the carpet, leaving a sprinkling of fresh dirt on the floor. She paid no heed to the mess.

"What did you say?" Janet asked in a throaty whisper.

"I know it's a juicy bit of gossip not to pass along to Bessie, but you promised. Personally, from what I saw of Georgia, I thought she was a little too phony. I prefer honest women like you."

"Oh," she said weakly.

"We were interrupted before he could tell me anything more when Georgia came into the room. I guess it's still a secret because he didn't mention it around her. She was practically purring over him. I suppose some men just go for that type," he concluded.

"That type?" she repeated vaguely.

"Sure. But then I don't have to tell you how it is between those two. Why when I was over at his ranch this morning, Georgia was all over him. She was hanging on his arm while he talked and giving him teasing little looks. Jason seemed a little anxious to be rid of me, probably so that he and Georgia could go back to doing whatever I had interrupted."

Janet's hand trembled as she held the receiver. So Jason had left her bed, after taking all she had to give and had given in love, to return to Georgia. Janet hadn't even concerned herself with the beautiful blonde last night, had even forgotten she existed, but Jason obviously had not. And after spending time in her arms he had returned to Georgia, probably secretly amused at Janet's innocence and total surrender.

A spark of pure fury ignited and spread through

her. Well, she was not a plaything to be used and discarded! There was no way to reverse the events of last night, but she would never allow it to happen again, she resolved with a stormy defiance. Jason Stewart, with his superior knowledge of women and how to arouse them, would never again get past the barrier she had just erected around him.

"Are you still there?" Ron asked.

"Yes." Her voice was brittle, "I'm still here."

"Good. Well, I thought we might go out next weekend."

"I'd love to," she said mechanically. But as she spoke her mind was whirling with other thoughts. Why should she stay in Freedom? She never wanted to see Jason again and she didn't want to be exposed to any chance meetings with him. Now was the time to leave.

"Fine. I'll talk to you before then, but I wanted to make sure you were free."

"Ron," Janet said, "I wonder if we couldn't go to Tulsa this weekend. I might as well pack up my things and go ahead and move."

He sounded surprised when he replied. "All right. I'll stop by tonight and we'll make plans for the trip."

"Good." Janet hung the phone up, forgetting to say good-bye. She stared out the window, seeing nothing of the robins hopping on the lawn or the geraniums growing in the window box. What she was was the sardonic face of a tall, rugged man whose eyes mocked her.

The night that had been so special to Janet had meant nothing to Jason. He probably had regretted from the start that Georgia had not been able to come and he had decided to substitute Janet. She felt hot tears sting her eyelids at that thought.

Yanking off the gardening glove she hurled it across the room. She was not going to cry for Jason Stewart. She stalked into her bedroom, pulled her suitcase from under the bed, and began taking her clothes from the closet. She was going to pack now and move to Tulsa immediately. There was no reason to stay here in Freedom. And the sooner she left the better she would feel.

She was in the midst of packing her kitchen things when the telephone sounded again. Janet picked it up and spoke crisply. "Hello."

"This is Jason Stewart," he identified himself unnecessarily.

"What do you want?" she shot at him.

"I thought we might go somewhere this Friday night, perhaps to dinner—"

Janet slashed through his words. "I'm busy."

"Well, perhaps Saturday."

"I am also busy on Saturday and any other night you might ask me out," she told him unequivocally. She slammed the receiver down.

The phone rang again while she was still staring dazedly at it. She picked it up and held it to her ear, saying nothing.

"Listen, Janet, I don't know what's wrong, but I think it's something we could talk out."

"If you ever," Janet said in a voice that shook with feeling, "call this number again, I will report you to the phone company for harrassment. Do you understand?"

The phone was dead.

All packing forgotten, Janet retreated back to her

room and indulged herself in a flood of tears. They abated slowly. When she finally pulled herself from the bed and surveyed her face in the bathroom mirror, the ravages of her crying binge were readily apparent in her red-rimmed eyes and tearstained cheeks. Damn Jason Stewart! She rammed a clenched fist into the open palm of her other hand.

Why had he called her? He must revel in torturing her. Did he have to prove once again that he could make her melt in his arms? Well, maybe he could, but she wasn't going to give him the chance. He had mocked her once too often. She would never, never see him again and she would be better off for it.

Whether or not she would be better off remained for the distant future to prove, but she was miserable for the next two days as she completed her packing. She took some of her plants down to Bessie's house as gifts for the older woman.

"So you're really going?" Bessie said, swinging her door open for Janet to enter carrying a brilliant purple African violet.

"I told you I was."

"I know," Bessie said, closing the door and indicating the end table as a place to deposit the plant. "But I kept a-thinking you would change your mind."

"No, I'm going."

"You'll be back to visit won't you?"

"Of course."

"And if there's a wedding, I'll expect to be invited." Bessie told her with a sly gleam in her blue eyes.

"Don't worry, there is no wedding in my future," Janet said in clipped accents.

"Sit down and have a cup of sassafras tea," Bessie invited.

"I'll help you fix it," Janet offered, following the old woman into her kitchen.

"When are you moving?"

"This weekend. I can leave my things at Ron's apartment until I find a place of my own and I'll be staying with a friend of his until then. It's a girl," she added with a laugh as Bessie raised a gray eyebrow.

"Well, I'll be sorry to see you go, but it's like I been a-telling you all along, this ain't no place for young people." Bessie handed Janet an empty glass. "Put some ice in there, will you hon?"

While Janet filled the glass Bessie mixed the tea. They carried the drinks back into the living room. "I'll give you Rita's address in Tulsa," Bessie said, seating herself on the aging brown sofa.

Janet smiled her thanks. She couldn't imagine ever being desperate enough to call on Rita, but she said nothing while Bessie wrote the name and address of her daughter on a piece of paper in a scrawling hand.

"Thanks," Janet accepted the address.

"Well," Bessie said, settling back on the couch. "I saw Susan Stewart with her uncle at the store the other day. She was asking about you."

Janet looked guiltily down at the floor. She had not seen Susan since her cliff-hanging episode, nearly four weeks ago. But then it would be a little awkward to visit Susan at Jason's house and just as awkward to have Jason drop his niece off at her house.

"I'll write her when I get to Tulsa," Janet said.

"That would be nice," Bessie said. "I think she sort of looks up to you like the mother she doesn't have."

Janet stood abruptly, putting her glass down on a coaster. "I've got to be going now. I'll stop by and see you before I leave."

"I'd like that."

Janet walked out the door and back to her house with a sobering sense of depression settling in. She had failed Susan. And she was failing Ron by leading him to believe there could ever be anything more to their relationship than the casual friendship they now shared. But worst of all, she thought, stepping into the house and looking at the boxes stacked around the living room, she was failing herself.

She had fled Indiana to escape the bad memories. And now she was fleeing Freedom to escape the painful memories of her unreturned love. She sank down on a chair and looked at the suitcases and grocery sacks standing beside the boxes, all signs of her departure. And what did she hope to find in Tulsa that she had not found here?

But there was no turning back now. She had accepted the post and she had given notice to her landlady in Freedom that she would be vacating the house. She would go to Tulsa and start over. And she would not flee Tulsa when things became unbearable there. She would learn to cope in Tulsa, but she could never learn to cope here. Not when she would be seeing Jason at frequent and unexpected intervals during the months and years ahead if she stayed.

CHAPTER 10

Janet let the curtain fall closed and transferred her attention from the winter street outside her window to the tranquil blandness of her apartment, lit with the twinkling lights of the Christmas tree that stood beside the television. In her hand she held a letter from Susan she had received that day.

Janet had written the little girl weekly letters since she had moved to Tulsa and Susan had responded with a letter-writing devotion rare in one so young. But this letter was the most disturbing one that Janet had yet received. The others had been bright little essays, scrawled on yellow pieces of blue-lined paper. But the letter that had been in her mailbox this evening was different.

The message was simple. Susan was inviting Janet to the ranch for Christmas. Janet bit her lip in concentration and let her hand fall lifelessly to her side. She could have disregarded the invitation and written a polite letter declining. But there were two problems. One was that Susan had not mailed the letter until four days before Christmas. As a result it had arrived only two days before the holiday and that did not give Janet time to respond by mail. But the second and most important reason that she was reluctant to deny Susan's request was that the letter had ended almost in a plea for Janet to come. How could she deny a child at Christmas? Images of Jason Stewart's house came to her mind. Susan's impersonal room and the impassivity with which Jason treated his niece also came into mind. It would be a lonely Christmas for Susan, she knew.

But could she go back? Could she spend a weekend in a house with a man she both loved and hated so fiercely? She made a wry face as she remembered how she had decided to forget Jason when she came to Tulsa.

She had made friends among the teachers at her school and she still saw Ron, although now they were more friends than a couple. He was also dating another girl. But the memory of the man in Freedom was too overpowering to be banished from her thoughts for any length of time.

Pulling on a coat, Janet ventured out into the evening wind, locking the door of her apartment after her. She did not usually walk the city streets at night, but in this quiet residential neighborhood she felt safe. And tonight she had to escape the confines of her little apartment. She needed time to think.

With her head bowed against the shrill December wind she started down the wide, tree-lined streets housing venerable old mansions that had been built by oilmen in the twenties. She glanced at a striking Georgian home as she walked past it. Red brick surrounded a pedimented door and perfectly symmetrical arched windows adorned either side of the entryway. Next to it a Tudor house of board and plaster drew her eye.

She slowed her steps and stopped to look at the

house. Inside the window she could see a fireplace mantel decorated with holly. Beside it a tree that went nearly to the top of the high-ceilinged room twinkled with thousands of tiny artificial candles.

Suddenly Janet felt a stab of loneliness. She had told Ron she had plans for Christmas and he had not pressed. She had none. The thought of spending the day by herself seemed hopelessly sad. And worse, the knowledge that a little girl would also be spending the day virtually alone made up her mind for her. She turned and started back toward her apartment. She would go to Freedom for Susan's sake. She would go and take the little stack of gifts she had bought for Susan and had never been able to bring herself to mail. Maybe she had known all along she was going to go.

Her resolution made, Janet returned to her apartment and began to pack, sorting through her clothes carefully. She finished and closed the lid of the suitcase, slipped out of her clothes and into her nightgown, and crawled into bed. But half an hour later she was still staring wide-eyed at the ceiling. In her growing excitement she could not sleep. The last conversation she had had with Jason kept returning to her mind, plaguing her with its ambiguity. It had done so ever since she had arrived in Tulsa. Jason had called to ask her out. Could he *really* have wanted to take her out? Had he not meant it only as a taunting gesture?

Her heart ached with the longing to discover herself mistaken about Jason. But the memories of other words between them and other actions from the bold, arrogant man could not support her thin hope. No, he was exactly as she thought him. He was uncaring of other people, even deliberately hurtful. How then, could she love him?

Janet was on the road at nine in the morning, having finally fallen into a peaceless sleep. Progress was slow. The weather was good. It seldom snowed in Oklahoma at Christmas, but the holiday traffic was out in full force. Consequently the drive to Freedom, normally only slightly over a three-hour drive from Tulsa, was drawn out to over five hours. She did not arrive in Freedom until after two in the afternoon and by the time Janet finally reached the turnoff to the ranch, it was after three.

Now the short winter day was drawing near a close and the sun was sinking gradually down toward the western prairie. Janet braked the car for a minute to watch the sunset in silent respect. How many primitive men, she wondered, had run westward to touch the ball of fire? It was so close and visible as the bottom edge of it neared the earth that it looked reachable.

She remembered another day when she had watched the sun rise with such majestic power. But the memory of that day also brought to mind the thought of her foolhardy climb up the cliff and Jason's rescue. She took her foot off the brake and drove on toward the house. She didn't want to dwell on the events of that day or the day that had followed.

She stopped in front of the Spanish-style house and walked to the door, rang the bell, and waited.

A moment later the door was opened by Rosa. "Come in," she said in a thick accent. "I will tell Susan you are here."

A minute later Susan was bounding down the hall

toward her. "I knew you'd come!" Susan greeted her breathlessly, hugging her swiftly. "I want to show you the tree in the den. It's huge! I helped decorate it." The little girl took her hand and started across the living room, pulling Janet after her.

"I'm sure it's very nice," Janet told her, laughing at Susan's possessive grip on her.

They stepped inside a room paneled with dark wood; one wall of it was given over to a stone fireplace. The tree stood in front of the fireplace. Susan scurried across the long room to plug in the lights of the tree.

"You're the fourth person to see it," Susan told her proudly, "only Hank and Rosa and I have seen it."

"What about your Uncle Jason?" Janet asked, unable to prevent the question from escaping her lips.

Susan's eyes dropped to the thick brown carpet on the floor. "We only put the tree up today and he isn't home."

"Where is he?"

Susan adjusted a bulb on the tree. "He went to Tulsa."

"Oh," Janet felt almost ill. She had driven all the way from Tulsa and Jason was not here. But she came to see Susan, she reminded herself grimly. Even as that thought went through her mind she knew it wasn't true. She had come to Freedom for one reason and that was to see Jason. She remembered with a touch of self-mockery how much time last night she had devoted to selecting her outfit before finally settling on the charcoal gray slacks and light gray lambswool sweater with a flattering cowl neck that she was wearing now. She had thought of Jason's reaction as she had put them on this morning and saw how they revealed her slender figure.

"Wh-When will he be back?" Janet asked. She wanted her voice to sound casual, but there was a cracking tone in it that she could not control.

Susan turned to her, forcing an artificial smile. "Come and see my room. I painted some pictures in art class to put on my walls and they look real nice."

Janet made no reply as she wordlessly followed Susan back to the little girl's room. She hadn't really needed to hear Susan answer her question. She knew Jason had gone to Tulsa to see Georgia and she also knew he would probably spend the holidays with her.

Susan threw the door to her bedroom open and Janet stepped into the room. Unaccountably, anger flared in her. "What of the pretty curtains and bedspreads you wanted to buy? Why didn't your uncle buy them for you?" she demanded.

Susan looked at her soft-spoken teacher in surprise. Janet moderated her tone. "Didn't your uncle buy you any of the things you wanted?"

"He might be giving them to me for Christmas," Susan suggested, disbelief of that wistful statement in her small voice.

"Of course he might," Janet assured her, not believing it for an instant. But this was Christmas Eve and there was no reason for her to upset Susan just because her own dreams had been shattered.

"Here's my best picture," Susan changed the subject, pointing to a childish portrait of Abraham Lincoln taped to the wall.

"How nice," Janet murmured.

"Yes," Susan agreed with simple pride. "And there's one of George Washington."

Janet smiled. The likeness to the nation's first president was less than striking. She was glad she had not been asked to guess who the portrait was since her first guess would have been Eleanor Roosevelt.

"And this," Susan pointed to a man on a horse beside a woman with long blond hair, "is Uncle Jason."

"Who's the woman?" Janet asked. It was a mechanical question. The woman was obviously Georgia—no other woman had such silky golden hair.

Susan's answer surprised her. "It's you. I drew it last summer."

"But I don't ride a horse," Janet said irrelevantly, "and I don't have blond hair."

Susan turned her face back to the picture. "You could learn to ride. Everyone out here rides. And last summer your hair was streaked blond in places with the sun. Maybe you could dye it," she suggested, "if Uncle Jason likes blond hair."

"Susan," Janet's voice was measured and taut, "I am not going to change myself to attract a man—any man. They will just have to take me as I am."

"You don't have to change yourself completely," Susan pleaded. "If you would make a few little changes and he would make a few changes, you could get along together."

"Life isn't like that. People rarely adapt to fit another person's image of what they should be. And it would be too late for me now, even if I wanted to," she added, speaking now as one adult to another.

"Yes," Susan admitted ruefully. "It would."

Janet was instantly alert, feeling her body tense. "What do you mean?"

"Uncle Jason said when he went to Tulsa that he would be married when he came back. He sounded sort of—" she paused, searching in her limited vocabulary for the right word to describe her uncle's words, "I don't know, he sounded almost mad when he said it."

"Mad?"

"Yes, he said she was going to marry him whether she wanted to or not. And his face was set hard like it gets when one of the field hands has crossed him and he wants to show who's boss."

Janet was paying scant attention to Susan's latter words. Her mind was occupied with trying to understand the first sentence. "Whether she wanted to or not? But surely Georgia would want to marry Jason."

"That's what he said," Susan affirmed, her voice sounding strained.

Janet looked down at the little girl's face. It was drawn and tired-looking. This was almost Christmas, she reminded herself, recalling all the happy Christmases she had spent as a child. There was no one else here to see to Susan's happiness so she must do it. Later, she could give herself over to the despair that was washing through her.

"Well," she interjected a false note of heartiness in her voice, "I have a whole carload of presents. I'll need some help carrying them in. We might even," she added with a smile, "find a present or two for you."

The little girl's concerns were forgotten in her new excitement. Susan and Janet carried in the luggage and presents from her car. After stowing her suitcases in a guest bedroom they placed the presents under the tree. Turning out the lights in the room, Susan lit the lights on the tree and they sang carols around it. They were joined by Rosa, whose grasp of the words was not good, but her strong, throaty voice added a hearty tenor to the evening.

Afterward they drank warm apple cider and freshly baked cookies.

"We can open the presents in the morning," Janet told Susan, wanting to leave something for the child to look forward to, "but it's nine o'clock now and I think it's time you were in bed. You have a big day ahead of you tomorrow with opening your presents, going to church, and a nice Christmas dinner." Janet had no idea what kind of dinner was planned, but she was going to make certain that it was special if she had to cook it herself.

Half an hour later Susan was tucked carefully in bed and Janet quietly closed the door of her room. Turning, she strolled listlessly back to the living room. Rosa had gone to her own room at the back of the house to watch television, leaving her alone. Janet turned off the lights in the living room and sat on the ocher sofa in the darkened room.

The thoughts that crowded into her mind required a dark and isolated place. Very near the surface was the avalanche of tears she was trying desperately to suppress. But the ache, the curious constriction in her throat, could not be suppressed. She swallowed hard, but the lump would not go down. She had never felt more completely shattered than she did right now.

Startled by a noise, Janet wrenched her head toward the door as it opened. A tall, masculine shape was outlined in it before it was closed again and the man stood in the room with her, his body shrouded in darkness.

"Don't turn the light on," she said, her voice soft in the velvet blackness.

There was a silence, so palpable it seemed touchable. "Janet?" Jason's disbelieving voice finally said.

She made no reply.

"Janet." His tone was surer now. "What are you doing here?"

"I came to see Susan." She spit the words at him.

"Oh."

What had his accent on the word implied? It had sounded almost like disappointment, but she could not be sure in the dark room. If the light were on, she would certainly discover that she was deceiving herself and that his face wore the same sardonic expression she was so used to.

"Are you married?" she hurled at him.

She heard his footsteps treading softly across the tiled floor toward her and then he seated himself in a chair close to her before he replied. "Married? Who told you I was getting married?"

"Susan did."

"Did she?"

Janet shifted uneasily on the sofa. She didn't like exchanging these short, noninformative sentences with a man whose face she could not see. But better than looking at his face. That, she knew, would be her complete undoing, and the tears waiting to spring forth would flow freely.

"Susan didn't tell me you were coming."

"She didn't know it. I only decided yesterday."

More silence. What was that unreadable quality in his voice? It did not match the arrogant man that Jason was. His tone almost lacked confidence. Had he been rejected in his pursuit of Georgia? Was that why he was so strangely brooding?

Janet phrased the question as if she had every right to ask it. "Did Georgia turn you down?"

"No."

"I see," she managed the words as large tears fell from her eyes, sliding down her cheeks and misting her brown eyes so that even the inkiness of the room was a murky, shifting shape.

In an instant Jason was beside her on the couch. "No," he repeated, "she didn't turn me down. I'm used to getting what I want." Cupping her chin in his hand he raised her face to his, finding her lips surely even in the undisclosing darkness of the room.

The lips that invaded hers were burning and agonizingly sweet. For a wild moment she answered his embrace with a fervor that was like a wildfire fanned out of control after smoldering for a very long time. But the thought of his words returned with the effect of a powerful extinguisher. He had said he was going to marry Georgia. He was also, as he had just said, used to getting what he wanted. Since Georgia was not with him now he would settle for Janet tonight.

Her trembling hands found their way to his chest and she pushed against him with a strength born of pain and bitterness. "Save your kisses for your wife." She said the last word with an accent of loathing.

Jason laughed softly and took her hands in his. Removing her ineffective hands from his broad chest he brought his face down to hers again. He kissed the

Jason continued unperturbed, stopping to brush a lock of her hair back. "After that our paths seemed to be constantly crossing. I was attracted to you—I knew that—but I didn't know how strongly until I starting becoming jealous of Ron Leonard. That's when I realized how badly I wanted you."

"Wanted me," Janet repeated uncertainly. Yes, he had desired her, she had known that all along. But that wasn't enough for her.

"I wanted you in a purely physical sense at first. I'm not a monk. The way you looked in some of those outfits was very appealing, with your long tan legs inviting me to explore further the temptations hidden by scanty tops and shorts. Still, there was something deeper that drew me to you. It was something I had never felt with any other woman and it frightened me."

"Why are you telling me these things? You're going to marry Georgia."

"Janet," Jason said, pulling her onto his lap and holding her there firmly as he wrapped his arms around her. "Georgia was a very 'giving' woman. No, don't try to move away." He chuckled and stopped to kiss her. "Where was I? Oh, yes, she and I had a very fulfilling relationship until you came along. After that my interest in her waned. I suppose the only reason I continued seeing her after I met you was because I refused to admit what you were to me. There's a lot more to tell you, but we can talk later. Right now I have something more pleasant in mind for us."

He didn't give her time to speak before his lips stroked hers invitingly and then opened to possess hers more fully. Unable to resist his offer, her own

tip of her nose before moving downward to the slender column of her neck.

"Stop it!"

"Why?" he murmured against her throat.

She jerked backward fiercely. "Why are you tormenting me?"

Jason draped a hand across her drooping shoulders. "I am not tormenting you, love. You have made me very miserable and you must now make me very happy to erase the pain you have caused."

"I-I don't understand," she stammered.

Jason leaned across her and flipped on the table lamp. Turning his ocean blue eyes back to her he started in surprise. "You've been crying. Why?"

"It doesn't matter," she said, standing and starting from the room.

Jason was beside her in a moment, halting her and turning her to face him. "I think we should sit down and talk this over." A smile played on his lips.

"There's nothing to discuss."

"Janet, don't argue with me. Although," he added with a boyish grin, "I must admit that making up is much nicer after a fight."

"We have nothing to make up about."

"Oh, yes we do." His tone was suddenly serious. "I think our relationship has been riddled with misunderstandings. I want you to sit down and we'll start at the beginning."

Janet allowed him to guide her back to the couch.

"First," he said, picking up one of her hands and stroking it as he spoke, "I thought you were trying to interfere in my personal affairs when you called me to school to discuss Susan."

Janet responded with spirit. "I wasn't."

lips parted pliantly and she felt the softness of his tongue lightly playing against the dark recesses of her mouth. She entwined her arms around his neck, giving herself over to the moment even though her mind was still trying to understand all of his words.

The fog deepened as his sure hand ran slowly up under her gray sweater to cup a warm breast, gently massaging it into a firm peak before moving over to the other one. Tantalizing fingers of delight ran up and down her spine and she felt an awakening desire that was fueled by the hard feel of him. He pushed her gently back. Her lips were swollen from the sensuous touch of his, and her breasts heaved, firm and demanding.

"Lord, you're beautiful," he whispered, burying his face in her long hair. "You'll be a beautiful bride."

Janet straightened. "Are you really asking me to marry you?"

"Yes," he replied in a husky whisper.

She studied him in confusion. "If you wanted to marry me, why did you let me leave Freedom?"

"I thought you made the choice to go with Ron. If he was the man you wanted, than I couldn't throw myself at you and beg you to take me. I have my pride, you know," he ended with dignity.

"You certainly do," she agreed tartly.

With a swift, fluid motion, he pulled her back onto his lap and imprisoned her arms against her sides with strong arms. "But you do too, Janet. I can imagine the satisfaction it gave you to reject my offer for a date and then hang up on me."

Janet recalled the incident with dismay. "You

really wanted to take me out," she recalled with wonder. "You weren't just tormenting me?"

He gave a short laugh. "I never wanted anything more in my life than to go out with you, to build on the unsteady friendship we were establishing."

"We could have been together so much longer if I had understood your feelings at the time."

"We could be together now if only you would give me an answer to my question," he reminded her. "Will you marry me?"

"Yes," she answered softly.

For a moment they merely looked at each other, as if they could see their future reflected in the other's eyes. Then they slowly bent their heads together and kissed in an unhurried, tender embrace. He drew back slowly.

"There's something I want to ask you," he said. "I realize this probably isn't the time, but it's been on my mind for a long while."

"What is it?"

"The man in the picture with you and your parents—who was he really? I mean, who was he to you?"

"I was engaged to marry him, but he died," Janet replied simply.

"How long ago was that?" he asked.

"It has been more than a year."

"Do you—" He stopped and then began again. "Are you still in love with him?"

Janet considered the question carefully before she replied. "Yes. I'll always love Lars. He was the first man who was really important to me. I think that was part of the reason I didn't want you to become special; I felt I would be betraying his memory."

"Is that how you feel now?" Jason probed.

"There's an innocence about a first love, especially about a lost one, that can never be regained." Janet looked past him as she spoke. "Now I know it's possible to love someone else just as strongly and as deeply, maybe even more so, because I have the wisdom of experience." She knew her words were true. The idyllic romance she had shared with Lars would have lessened when the realities of life had edged in; it was inevitable. With Jason she was beginning with a true picture of the struggles that lay ahead as well as the joys.

"I want to make you happy," Jason said wistfully.

"You will." She paused. "I love you," she added softly, looking into his eyes as she spoke.

There was no need for further talk. He reached over and turned off the light. "Let's go to bed," he murmured as he rose and helped her up. Janet followed him through the darkened halls of the house. He led the way unerringly to his bedroom and closed the door behind them. Then he took her hand again and guided her to the bed.

It seemed to Janet as if everything afterward happened in slow motion. His hands moved over her body very gently, touching the curves of her body, before coming to rest on the alluring crevice in the valley between her breasts. After he freed them of their confinement, Janet felt his mouth exploring the tips of her breasts and then returning upward to her throat. Her head was flung back in abandon as she savored his touch. It had been so long and she had ached so badly for him. A feeling of safety flooded through her and she murmured his name as he brought his lips to hers.

This was the night she had dreamed of, but had never expected to come true. He was on the bed beside her, leading her back into the realms she realized she could enter only with him. She could smell the woodsy scent of his aftershave, touch the firm feel of his skin, and hear the rhythm of his unsteady breathing; she delighted in every aspect of him.

Everything about Jason was the same as the last time they had been together—and nothing was the same. He loved her. She knew what she had never dared hope before. That knowledge freed her to give even more of herself than she ever had.

Her breathing deepened as he explored her body with sensitive hands. The excitement that had been growing within her began to reach a peak of anticipation. Then he was totally hers and she felt both a relaxation and a new tenseness. This was the perfect moment, she thought, even as she felt her yearning building. She was like a runner, racing faster and faster, moving forward to something she couldn't quite see through a mist. She didn't even know what she was running toward, but she would know when she reached it.

She realized Jason sensed the urgency within her as he murmured soft words into her ear. She couldn't understand the words, but she knew the intent of them. Then she didn't hear anything at all as a wave washed over her. She had reached her goal and she felt a blissful sense of exhilaration. A soft moan of pleasure escaped her. She had forgotten how good it would feel, she considered as the sensuous waves of ectasy washed over her again and again. Jason held her tightly in his arms as she subsided back to reality.

The silence between them was unbroken until both

of their ragged heartbeats settled into a steady pace. "I hope it can always be like that," Janet whispered, still clutching him.

He made no reply as he stroked the tingling skin along her spine.

"Jason," she began as she lay back slowly on the bed, "I want to talk about—"

"Shhh," he silenced her with a finger on her lips. "We'll talk in the morning. Now go to sleep."

"Bully," she muttered as she laid her head against the soft hair on his chest and closed her eyes.

When she opened them again, she blinked against the light and then looked up slowly. Jason was lying on the bed beside her, watching her. "Good morning," he smiled when she blinked again. He reached out a hand and stroked her naked thigh beneath the covers.

"What time is it?" she asked groggily.

"Five thirty," he replied.

She closed her eyes. "I'm going back to sleep. Wake me up at a civilized hour."

"Oh no, you're not," he laughed. "There are things I want to say to you that we didn't discuss last night."

"I was busy then," she bantered.

"I want to talk about Ron," he said, suddenly serious.

Janet looked at him steadily. "Yes?"

"You left with him to go to Tulsa."

"Ron," she began, "is a wonderful person. I think he deserves a really special girl and I hope he finds one. But I wasn't that woman. I guess my mind was always too occupied with you to ever allow another man in." She noted the look of disbelief on his face. "Hard to believe, isn't it?" Janet teased as she raised herself to a sitting position and tossed her head back to free it of the hair tumbling forward. "It's funny, but I was always aware of you. I'm not sure when I fell in love with you, but I can tell you I didn't intend to."

"I can believe that," he replied with a laugh. "You certainly didn't seem to be trying to worm your way into my good graces when *I* was around you."

"I suppose you were trying to win me?" she asked archly.

He gave a rueful smile. "No, I wasn't. I spent so damn much time trying to convince myself you meant nothing to me that I'm surprised I got anything else done."

"You seem to have found time for Georgia," she noted.

He leaned over and gave her a quick, firm kiss on the mouth. "We can talk about that later," he said as he pulled her closer toward him.

She slid out of his arms. "Oh no, we'll talk now."

"All right," He grinned. "I did find time for her. I hoped she could make me forget you, but it didn't work. I'm no longer seeing her and I won't be in the future."

"That's good," Janet said dryly. "I don't know how I could explain to our friends that my husband was dating a ravishing blonde."

"You know," he continued thoughtfully, "when I first met you, I thought you looked so young that for a time I didn't want to become involved with you because of the age difference."

"What changed your mind?"

"You didn't act that young. You seemed more mature than the twenty-one year-old girl you looked to be. A few carefully worded questions to Susan gave me the information I needed. I was relieved to find out you were twenty-six."

"Snoop," she commented.

"Yes," he agreed placidly. "Speaking of Susan, there is something you don't know about the night she ran away. I started to tell you once, but you didn't seem inclined to listen at the time."

"I am now."

"When I returned to the ranch from your house after Susan had been found, I was upset. I felt like some sort of monster that a seven-year-old had run away to escape me. I guess that was when I had my first real talk with her." He paused and then continued hesitantly. "I realized after that discussion how much truth there was to what you had tried to tell me when you called me into your classroom. Susan *was* having a lot of problems. Part of her blamed her parents for dying and leaving her alone in a world of strangers, and another part of her refused to believe they were really dead. I know it sounds paradoxical; it is. But she thought she should go back to New Jersey and look for them. Anyway," he finished, "she was an unhappy child."

"So what did you do?" Janet probed, pulling the cover up around her as she sat up in bed.

"I took her to New Jersey. I had to prove to her that they were dead as much as to show her that I was available for her. We spent some time there; I took her to her old school and she saw friends and neighbors. We developed a kind of rapport. I realized for the first time that my responsibility toward her was more than just providing her meals and a place to live." He stopped.

Janet ran her fingers across the smooth brown sheets. "Go on," she prompted when he did not speak again.

Jason shrugged. "There's really nothing more to tell. Susan didn't entirely trust me from the start and she sure as hell didn't like or trust Georgia. She thought we would be getting married and the idea frightened her. She was willing to do whatever she could to stop that union. That," he added as he put an arm around Janet and drew her toward him, "was the part where she kept trying to throw us together. When you left after spending the day here and Georgia stayed, Susan saw it as the defeat of her plans; she was sure I was going to marry Georgia."

Recalling Susan's words of yesterday, Janet noted. "Apparently Susan still thinks you intend to marry Georgia. That's why she thought you went to Tulsa."

He looked faintly surprised. "I never thought she would consider that since I haven't been seeing Georgia. She'll be glad of the change," he said with a smile. "Our marriage will be the little matchmaker's fondest dream come true."

"I'm glad. By the way," she continued. "What did you get her for Christmas?"

At that he laughed outright. "So she's still hinting at every turn for those curtains. I got them for her and the bedspread too."

"That should make her happy."

"Let's talk about us for a while," he changed the subject with a provocative look at the curves revealed beneath the covers.

"All right," she said with a teasing glance through demurely lowered lashes, "I like hot chocolate and scrambled eggs for breakfast and I like them served in bed."

He stood and wrapped a wine velour robe about himself. "It's your turn tomorrow," he noted as he walked from the room.

LOOK FOR NEXT MONTH'S CANDLELIGHT ECSTASY ROMANCES™:

28 STAGES OF LOVE, *Beverly Sommers*
29 LOVE BEYOND REASON, *Rachel Ryan*
30 PROMISES TO KEEP, *Rose Marie Ferris*